Chasing Glory

A CURVY GIRL AGE GAP INSTALOVE PRISON ROMANCE

DANGEROUS CURVES AHEAD
BOOK ONE

LIA PRESTON

LUNARIA PRESS, INC.

FIRST EDITION

PAPERBACK **ISBN**: 978-1-7388946-7-3

Cover: Lunaria Cover Design
Editing: Eyes on Your Story

PUBLISHED IN CANADA BY LUNARIA PRESS, INC.

Chapter One

Chase

"Franklin."

I grunted as the sound of my name broke through my sleep.

"You're coming with me," Victor Davis, one of the guards, said as he shook my shoulder.

"For what?" I croaked out, my voice hoarse from the stale cell air. It was too early in the morning for this shit.

It'd been a rowdy night. As it always was when we were confined in our cells for too long. We'd been on lockdown since yesterday because they'd caught someone with a cell phone in our unit. Some of the inmates were like baboons at the zoo, hooting and hollering for attention anytime a guard passed by. I'd barely slept.

"You have anger management."

I turned over in my bunk to face the wall. "Pass."

Anger management? What the fuck for? That was for

people who didn't know how or when to act. I had zero regrets for doing what I'd done to my sister's cheating piece-of-shit husband. They'd be disappointed if they were expecting me to have remorse for hitting the guy. My only regret was that I hadn't stood up for her sooner.

The guard, Officer Victor Davis, otherwise known as V.D. by the inmate population, poked me in the back. "It's mandatory."

I heard Lucian stir in the bunk below me. "Shit, Chase, just go, you prick. You're disturbing my beauty sleep."

I chuckled. Luc was the only guy in the place that I could tolerate, he was ex-military, like me, and he was a grumpy mother fucker if he didn't get enough sleep, then again, so was I. I wasn't sure what he'd done to end up in the same position as me, and I wasn't about to ask, but he seemed like a decent enough guy.

"Fine, fine." I sat up and hopped down. "It's bad enough that I have to look at your ugly face daily. If it gets any uglier…" I blew a raspberry into the air. "I don't think I could even stand it."

He groaned, "You wish you were as pretty as me."

The guy wasn't lying, he was handsome, but I'd been told I wasn't too shabby myself.

I pushed at his shoulder because he was looking a little too peaceful in his bed. "Keep talking about how pretty you are in here and someone's bound to take notice."

"Is that your way of asking me to call you Daddy, bro? Because if that's your aim, you'll have to buy me a lot of commissary first."

I couldn't help but laugh at that. Still, as much shit as we talked, we had each other's backs in here. Our jabs kept me sane by helping to pass the time. It was the time that was the worst. I'd never been one to sit idle for too long and it grated on my every nerve to have nowhere to go and nothing to do. I'd already served half of my sentence, but the last half was dragging on.

Davis shook his head at our antics as he left the cell and turned to wave me on. "Come on, Franklin, we ain't getting any younger. You can continue your lover's quarrel later."

I followed him through the cell door and he clicked it closed behind us before leading me to a few other inmates gathered in the middle of the room.

One guy caught my eye while I scanned the group. Yeah, he was the kind of bastard that needed anger management, not me. I'd overheard him threaten to shank a guy if he didn't give him his packet of jelly the other day. Or maybe it was the guy dangling it in his face and saying, 'I don't think you're ready for this jelly'. Either way, sugar was like currency in the joint. It was crazy how riled up they got over the tiniest of things.

But I guess, sometimes, the little things are all a guy's got.

It's better than nothing.

I should know. Since my dishonorable discharge from the military, that's all I've got.

Nothing.

I sat down in the circle with the other inmates. The chair was tiny and a long way down. Were they trying to humiliate us further?

There was no way I was going to be sharing any of my thoughts with these guys around. If I didn't have a parole hearing coming up, I wouldn't have been entertaining it at all. But I wanted to get out, of course I did. Shaving a year off of my sentence would be great.

The door to the room creaked open, and I sat back and folded my arms across my chest. I was prepared for some old grizzled-looking doctor. Maybe with an accent and a comb-over, and most likely a gut.

What I was not expecting was a woman like *her*.

I clenched my jaw as the cute and curvy girl walked into the room. She was tall, around five-foot-ten, but her figure was full and she'd pulled her hair back into a bun. A few tendrils had fallen loose, framing her face and tickling her neck. At least, I imagined they would tickle. The skin of her neck was pale and smooth, and there was a little cluster of dark freckles that almost formed a star pattern if only there was one more. I scanned her face. The star's last point was right above her glistening, juicy lips. It reminded me of where Marilyn Monroe had her beauty mark.

One guy let out a wolf whistle, and I snapped my head to see it was the jelly man. Stubbles, they called him, if my memory served me correctly. It was because he couldn't stop chewing his damn fingernails and they looked red and raw.

Nasty fucker.

I looked back at the doctor, who seemed unphased by him. Maybe she was used to these assholes? She looked young, too young to be working in a place like this. What was she thinking?

She scanned us all, her gaze locking with mine for a moment before she continued to her seat. "Sorry, I'm late. We weren't supposed to meet until the afternoon, but the guards pulled you all early."

Of course, they did. If they could exercise power and inconvenience us in the process—they would.

"I'm Dr. Gloria Moore. I'll be facilitating this anger management program. As we work through the exercises together, I'm hoping that we'll all be able to dig deep, identify our individual triggers, and develop some coping mechanisms that will serve us well when we're on the outside. We'll be meeting twice a week. Do you guys want to meet in the mornings or in the afternoons?"

Stubbles piped up, "I don't mind getting *it* up early for you, Doc."

I narrowed my eyes and my hands balled into fists as I stared at the sick fuck. He was getting on my nerves.

The guy sitting next to him hooted and slapped him on the shoulder, and a few other guys chuckled.

She looked away. "Does anyone else have a preference?"

"Afternoons," I said.

Her eyes went wide when she looked at me. The corner of her lip twitched into a grin. "And you'd be?"

"Franklin, Chase Franklin."

She scribbled something down. "Got it, Chase. Thanks for your input. Did you want to start off our introductions? Tell us a bit about why you're here in anger management?"

Not in the slightest, no.

But there was a pleading in her eyes that said she'd found a safe place with me. There were a couple of guards in the room, ready to protect her if anything went south, but she wasn't looking at them. Out of all the men in the room, it was me her bright blue eyes were looking at as they silently begged for refuge. Because of that, there was no way I was about to deny the beautiful Doctor anything she asked of me.

I groaned, sitting forward. "Sure, I'm Chase, I—" I scratched at my head. "—I'm here because… I, well, I don't have an anger management issue. My sister had an *asshole* problem, and I fixed it."

She noted something down and smiled at me. "Great, thanks for breaking the ice, Chase." As she worked her way through the rest of the introductions, I couldn't help but wonder what she had written down. What was so notable about what I'd said?

I bet even she would have rooted for me if she'd met Paul, my sister's ex-husband, or had seen how he treated her for years. Yeah, maybe I'd snapped, but it was a long time coming, and even though it cost me everything, I'd do it again. Liberty was my baby sister, and I'd protect her with all that I had. No matter what the consequences were for me.

That's what the sexy doctor would have to see in time. Unlike the yahoos surrounding me, I was there because sometimes you've gotta do what you gotta do to make sure that the people you love are safe from harm.

No amount of counseling could change my mind about that.

But I was all for letting her try—if only because it meant I got to spend more time with her.

Because now that I'd met her, I couldn't explain why, but I needed to make sure I was there for her.

Chapter Two

Gloria

The first session went a lot smoother than I'd imagined. A couple of the guys gave me the creeps, but I'd expected as much when I signed up to offer mental health counseling to inmates. There was only one that caught my eye for a different reason.

Chase Franklin.

He was handsome in a rugged sort of way. According to his file, he was ex-military, and he'd maintained the physique to prove it. They'd charged him with assault and sentenced him to two years. Although he wore an orange jumpsuit like the rest of them, he didn't seem to belong.

When the session was over, I told them to help themselves to coffee and bagels. The prison had brought them in before breakfast, but even though I assumed he must have been hungry too, Chase stayed in his seat. Maintaining distance from the rest of them.

I sat down next to him. "You're not hungry?"

He looked at me out of the corner of his eyes. In this light, they were a bright brown, almost amber. "I can wait until lunch."

The way he scanned my body warmed me. It wasn't predatory like some other inmates had been, but there was a visible interest in his eyes. If he was attempting to conceal his attraction, he was failing.

He cleared his throat. "You shouldn't have taken this job."

"What do you mean by that?"

"This place," he dropped his voice, "it's no place for a woman like you."

I smiled at him. It was easy to understand where he was coming from. "With all due respect, Chase, I'll decide when and where I'm needed."

He rubbed at the back of his neck, his biceps bulged as he did. He was a big guy, big enough to toss me over his shoulder whether I liked it or not. I stirred in my seat. Why had I thought that? It was inappropriate, and I'd never thought about a patient that way before. What was wrong with me?

Maybe I'd just been single for too long. My ex hadn't left me wanting to explore a romantic relationship with anyone else for a good long while. And I wasn't the kind to have sexual encounters outside of a commitment.

Chase grinned at me and a singular deep dimple appeared on his cheek. There was a kind of mischievous look about him when it revealed itself. "If you were *my* woman, you wouldn't be coming to a place like this."

I shot a quick glance at the guards. The coffee and bagels had everyone too distracted for them to overhear him. "Mr. Franklin, that's not an appropriate thing to say."

He waved his hand at me. "That's not how I meant it.

I'm just saying. That the man in your life shouldn't be letting you come here. Prison is full of predators, and I'm not just talking about the inmates."

"There's no man in my life, but even if there were, it wouldn't be up to him. And they're not all predators."

His head tipped back as he regarded me more directly. "Aren't they?"

"Are you?"

"Well, no, but—"

"I rest my case."

He chuckled. "Fair enough, Dr. Moore."

"You can call me Gloria. I appreciated you speaking first, but you were pretty closed off the rest of the time. First sessions can be a little intimidating, but I hope you'll relax a bit more next time so we can get to know one another better."

"Intimidating? Is that what you think? That I'm intimidated? You've got it all wrong, Dr. M—I mean—Gloria."

"If it's not that, what is it?"

He leaned forward, and my heart leaped in my chest. He locked his eyes on mine. "I'm in the wrong place. Anger implies you're not in control. And if you knew me, Gloria, you'd know that I'm *always* in control—always."

A surge of heat, that had no business existing, ran through me and pooled in the pit of my stomach. His dominant demeanor was intoxicating, or toxic, given our situation. I hopped out of my chair. I needed to regain control over the conversation and my reaction to it.

"Well, Mr. Franklin. People who are in control rarely end up in your shoes. I hope in time we'll uncover the reasons behind what happened so you don't end up here again."

His eyes narrowed at me. "Or *in time,* I'll show you how in control I am."

I sucked in a sharp breath. The way the words dripped off his tongue hinted at a hidden meaning behind them. Blood rushed to my head, and other areas I'd never imagined it would while at work. I clamped my thighs together as though that might stop me from reacting to him or his words.

I'd made a grave error in judgment.

Chase Franklin wasn't the safest man in the room.

He was the most *dangerous* of all.

Chapter Three

Chase

I couldn't get Gloria out of my mind. The way she squirmed when I pushed back at her attempt to dominate me consumed my thoughts.

If we'd met under different circumstances, she wouldn't stand a chance. I'd have already made her mine. She'd know without question just how in control I was.

Luc came into the cell. "So, how was therapy? Are you less of a dickhead yet?"

I looked at him out of the corner of my eye and smiled. "I just might be."

He tipped his head and approached my bunk. "Okay, that's not what I was expecting to hear. What happened? Your face crater of a dimple is showing, so it must be something good."

Oh, it was 'something good' all right, but it was also a

fucking pointless fantasy. I couldn't have a woman like Gloria. And not just because she was my doctor, and I was an inmate. I couldn't have her because she was too fucking perfect, and I had nothing of value to offer her in return.

Okay, maybe not *nothing*.

My cock was big enough that I could fuck her so good I'd leave her weak and quivering with desire. But that was about all I had going for me while locked up. There's no way I'd satisfy a woman like her—a doctor, no less—with that alone.

Still, I was struggling to fight the urge to claim her. But the question was, how?

"Fuck man, look at you. I asked you a question and you're fucking daydreaming instead of answering me."

Shit, I was, wasn't I?

I pushed myself up to a seated position and hopped off the bunk and chuckled. "You got me there, brother."

"That's it?"

I slipped on flip-flops and grabbed my toiletry bag. "Gotta go shower. I'll catch you later."

He'd get it out of me, but it was fun leaving him to wonder for a little while.

I stepped into the shower stall, letting the door swing closed behind me, and draped my towel over it. The luke-warm water poured over me.

Damn it, what I wouldn't do for a hot shower.

I always tried to get in there early while there was still some heat left, but the morning detour to anger manage-ment had prevented that.

The way Gloria hopped out of her chair, as though my

words had set it—or parts of her—on fire, echoed through my mind. I looked down at my naked body, my cock half-hard at the thought of her.

It had been so easy to shut off this part of myself in prison. But seeing her twice a week was going to make it tough to maintain. I palmed my erection, giving it a few slow strokes, and it grew eager as I imagined us alone.

No guards.

No other inmates.

Just the two of us.

How I'd pull her into my lap and, with her skirt riding high, thrust my cock deep into her. The shower warmed up a little more, and as it ran over my length, I imagined it was her pussy surrounding me—warming me. My strokes sped up as I thought about her hips swiveling in my lap as she ground against me.

Fuck, what I wouldn't give to be buried inside her.

I was so close. I placed my palm on the wall and leaned my head back, closing my eyes.

Her lips. I wanted to kiss them. Better yet, watch my cock disappear into her hot mouth as she stretched them around me. That was it. I was about to come.

A shock of ice-cold water hit my body and my head snapped forward. Two voices came from over by the sink.

Fuck.

As quickly as my dick went hard for her, it fell as my reality came back into focus. The moment was lost. I dropped it, finished showering and grabbed my towel.

I could hear the inmates by the sink talking but I didn't pay it much mind until I heard the one say, "That fucking doctor, man, her pussy might be fat, but it's still pussy. I'd fuck her."

I clenched my teeth, thankful I had strong enamel or

they might have snapped from the pressure. Apparently, I wasn't the only one having fantasies about Gloria. I didn't like the way he spoke about her, though. She was perfection. Then again, he was probably just a short-dick motherfucker that wouldn't know what to do with that much woman.

I heard a grating chuckle.

Stubbles.

I pulled on clean underwear and a jumpsuit.

"She was talking to V.D. about one-on-one sessions. I'm putting my name in. And when I get her alone, I'll give it to her. A bitch like that's gotta be desperate," Stubbles said.

The other guy laughed. "You're fucking dreaming, man. What makes you think she'll want your grubby cock? You haven't fucking showered in weeks."

Stubbles chuckled again. The man had no self-respect for sure. He didn't even mind being the brunt of the joke. It's dirty bastards like him that just might make good on their filthy ideas.

"It doesn't matter." He raised the pitch of his voice. "No, stop," he said in a mock-feminine voice. I opened the door to the shower. He slapped the counter in rapid succession, mimicking a sex clap while moaning like a woman. Before he dropped his voice back to normal. "Take. This. Ho," he said, punctuating his words with pelvic thrusts.

My hands balled into fists.

"You're fucking crazy," the other guy said.

"No, I just know that no means yes."

I'd heard enough.

I burst out of the shower stall and rushed him, slamming him into the counter before grabbing him by the collar of his jumpsuit. "What did you just say?"

"Wha—what the fuck! You better get your hands off me," Stubbles said.

The other guy took a few steps back, putting his hands up in surrender. He didn't want any part of it. *Smart guy.* I'd have taken them both down if I had to.

I stared down Stubbles. "You'll stay away from Gloria. Do you hear me?"

"Gloria?" He laughed in my face. "Do you hear this guy?" He looked over at the other guy. "Using her first name and defending her honor like he's her knight in shining armor or some shit." He pushed at my chest. "You can't defend a pussy that ain't even yours, *Soldier Shitbag,*" he spat.

"I can from the likes of you." Anger seethed through me as I stared him down. I had to let him go. No good could come of this. My grip on him tightened.

He laughed. "Look at this guy. Ooh, so intense. I can't tell if he wants to fight me or fuck me."

I wanted to pop that smug look right off his face so fucking bad. But I just gave him another shove against the counter and let go. "Stay away from her, or else. Understand me?"

As long as he stayed away from Gloria, he wasn't worth losing my chance at freedom.

I gathered my things from the shower stall.

"Or else what?"

I stopped and turned to look at him. "Or else you'll be slurping jelly through a straw for weeks."

He smirked at me. "Nah, I'll just get your girlfriend to breastfeed me."

That's it.

I dropped my clothing on the floor and launched at him, slamming my fist into his jaw with an audible crack. He started wailing and throwing wild punches at my chest.

We ended up on the floor. I was on top of him, feeding

him punches, when three guards grabbed me and pulled me off of him.

I heard Davis yell to one of the other guards.

"Take Franklin to the hole."

Chapter Four

Gloria

I made it through another session. Chase was not in attendance and neither was Ike Stubbington. Ike I could do without. The guy gave me the absolute creeps. But Chase, I'd expected to return after our exchange the other day as inappropriate as it may have been. I felt like there was something between us. Even though nothing could happen, I had grown attached to the idea of having him around.

I guess I was wrong.

Victor Davis sauntered over to me. "Axel was right about you working here, huh? Bad fucking idea, Gloria. You should've just listened to your old man."

I sighed. "He's not 'my old man,' Vic." This was the problem with dating bikers. Once you were claimed, that was that. Good luck getting the guy to leave you alone. Vic wasn't a part of the motorcycle club, but he was affiliated, that was for sure. I was sure they used him to sneak stuff to their guys on the inside. "Besides, what are you talking about?"

The session had gone pretty well. A few of the guys had opened up. There were some raw stories being shared, and I was feeling proud of what we'd accomplished as a group.

"You didn't notice a couple of missing guys?"

"Of course, I did."

"They got into a tussle over who was going to fuck you first."

"I doubt that's accurate."

"No, I swear to you." He nodded, agreeing with himself. "Franklin roughed up Stubbington real well. The guy's got a broken jaw, among other injuries."

"Where's Ch—Franklin now?"

Vic tipped his head. "What do you care?"

"He's my patient."

"Well, not now. His parole hearing was canceled. I'm sure they'll cancel his anger management too."

"They can't do that to him. If what you said happened really went down, he needs this more than ever. I'll have a word with Warden Johns."

Victor tutted. "Gloria, don't go getting attached to the inmates now. I wouldn't want to have to tell Axel how concerned I am about you."

I ignored his thinly veiled threat to report back to my ex-boyfriend. "How long is he going to be in the hole? A few days? A week?"

He laughed. "He put a guy in the hospital. Broke his jaw. Made him bleed. He's not going to see the light of day for at least a month."

I took a few steps back, picked up my bag, and stuffed

my notepad into it. "I see. Well, I've gotta run, Vic. See you on Tuesday."

One of the other guards opened the door for me and escorted me down the hall. Once I was through the one set of secured doors, I should have turned left to exit the building, but instead, I turned right and headed straight to the warden's office.

If Chase was in the hole, he was isolated. What would a month of that do to his mental health? Certainly no favors.

I knocked on the warden's door.

What exactly was my plan here?

Warden Johns opened her door and smiled at me. "Hey, Gloria. Is everything all right?"

She stepped back and waved me into her office. "Yes, well, no."

We sat down at her desk. "What's the problem? Are the sessions not going well? I know these guys can be a bit much to handle but—"

"No, it's not that. I'm wondering about an inmate that was missing from the group today. Chase Franklin. Victor told me he's been sent to the hole for fighting?"

"Oh yes, I'll be candid because it's just us here. Stubbington is vile. There was another inmate present when it all went down that confirmed much of Franklin's account of the event. Under different circumstances, I'd have been rooting for him."

"What happened?"

"Umm." She pursed her lips.

I was overstepping, and I knew it. "I mean, Victor told me that it involved me in some way. I was hopeful when I met Mr. Franklin that we'd be able to make great progress together. I've heard that you've canceled his parole hearing. Is that true?"

"Stubbington was making sexual comments about you while Franklin was present. Once he's recovered, because of the vulgarity of the comments made, he won't be returning to your sessions. While I understand why Franklin may have reacted, he has been charged with assault on another inmate. Given the severity of the injuries, he's looking at another six months. I've marked him down for another parole hearing at what would have been the end of his sentence. As long as nothing like this happens again, he should be able to get out on probation at that time. But for now, he's out of luck."

"Let me work with him."

"He'll be allowed to return to the anger management program once he's out of isolation."

"I don't think the group sessions are going to benefit him. There's a significant divide between him and the other inmates. You said I could have one-on-one sessions with some inmates if I thought they needed them, right?"

"I did, yes."

"Well, he needs them. Let me work with him."

"I don't see why not. Once he's out of isolation, you can set up your first session with him."

I didn't want to wait that long.

"Can I not begin sooner?"

"That's not something that's really done."

"I understand that. But I'm worried about what a month in solitary confinement is going to do to him. If you give me the chance to speak with him once or twice a week. We could make the time he spends in isolation work in favor of his rehabilitation instead of in opposition to it."

She sat back in her chair and looked up at the ceiling.

"He's a veteran, Warden Johns, not a criminal. I realize he did what he did to end up here in the first place, but there's no reason to believe he can't leave here as a normal functioning member of society with the necessary guidance. I know you're focused on rehabilitation above all else. It's why I chose to work here. If we don't act fast, we may fail him. We may make things so much worse."

"True." She chewed at her lower lip. "Fine. I'll grant you access to one-on-one sessions with him on one condition."

"What's that?"

"You keep it quiet. I'm already a woman working in a man's world and coming under fire for many of the programs I've implemented here—yours included. I can't have it getting around that I've gone too soft."

"You have my word."

She leaned forward and rested her arms on the desk. "A lot of people around here believe that prison is punishment, and while that may be true for some of the inmates here, it isn't for all of them. I don't want the ones who it isn't true for slipping through the cracks. But I'm walking a tightrope for it, you know?"

"I know you are. I'll keep it quiet, but what about the guards I'll encounter in the unit?"

"I'll do a little shuffling around and make sure I have ones I can trust present."

"Thanks, Warden." I stood. "I appreciate your attention on this matter. I'll let you get back to work."

She smiled and grabbed a stack of files from the corner of her desk and picked up her reading glasses before perching them on the tip of her nose. "No problem. Do me proud, Dr. Moore."

"Yes, ma'am, I will."

As I left the prison, my body was practically humming. I felt like I'd just committed a crime and got away with it. What had I just done? Had I forgotten my exchange with Chase? Or the way my body responded to him when he spoke about control? I'd just fought to be alone with him at least once a week. My argument for it was obviously convincing enough.

But there was one thing I wasn't convinced I could do. Trust in myself. Or, at least, in my ability to resist him. *I'd have to find a way.*

Chapter Five

Chase

Ninety-eight.

Ninety-nine.

One-hundred.

I pushed off the floor, done with my morning push-ups, and sat on the bed.

What now?

I'd been in solitary for a week. It was the same fucking thing every day. If I thought it was bad in the general population, I was wrong. Sure, there were tons of assholes I didn't miss, though, I missed shooting the shit with Lucian.

But it was worth it.

If I was right, I was pretty sure I'd done enough damage to Stubbles that he wouldn't be out of the infirmary for quite some time.

The door clicked open and V.D. walked in.

What the fuck was he doing here?

"Miss me?" he asked with a laugh.

I went to stand. "Am I heading back already?"

He shook his head. "Not a chance, Franklin. You have a visitor."

A visitor? In solitary confinement?

What the fuck was going on?

With an awful scraping noise, Gloria stepped around the corner and into my cell, dragging a chair behind her. I hopped up and stepped toward her to help.

"Sit back down, Casanova," Davis ordered.

"Well, you help her then." I pointed at the chair.

"I'm oka—," she said when he tore the chair from her grip, lifted it, and set it down further in the cell with a clatter.

Davis crossed the room. "Stand up."

"Why?"

"Just stand up, Franklin." He pulled the pair of handcuffs from his hip.

Gloria leaned forward in her chair to see what he was up to. "Vic, that's unnecessary."

Vic?

Did these two know each other well?

"He's an inmate, Gloria, you need to remember that. Axel would have my head on a pike if he heard I let you in this room alone with a prisoner, without measures being taken for your safety."

Axel?

Who the fuck was Axel?

I didn't know any guard by that name.

Okay, these two must've known each other outside of the prison. But why would a woman like Gloria have anything to do with V.D.? Or a guy named Axel, of all things...

She let out a huff. "Fine, just get out of here. You're eating up the hour."

Davis left the room, clicking the cell door closed behind him.

I sat back down on the bed across the room from Gloria. "Do you want to explain what's going on here?"

"They didn't tell you?"

I shook my head. "Informing inmates isn't high on their list of priorities."

"I'll be continuing your anger management one-on-one from now on. But let's call it counseling, because I think we should dig a little deeper."

"I'm not interested in digging deep, Gloria. I've already told you why I did what I did. That's all there is to it."

"Yes, I might have believed that a week ago. But now you've done it again."

"Because he deserved it too."

"What makes you think you get to decide who deserves what?"

"What makes you think working in a men's prison is a good idea for a woman like yourself?"

"Chase—"

I tipped my head at her. "Gloria."

She burst out laughing. "I don't know if I've ever met someone as bull-headed as you."

I smiled at her. "Aww, do you say that to all your patients?"

"No, only you."

"To what do I owe the honor?"

"You're a—well, you're different from the others. Because you…" she trailed off, wringing her hands together.

"And you're cute when you're flustered. Do I make you nervous?" I pointed at her hands with my chin.

Fucking handcuffs.

She dropped her hands to her sides. "Nervous? No, not at all. Why would you ask a thing like that?"

Her cheeks grew flush. It was such a sweet-looking pink. Like cotton candy. Fuck, she was delectable. But even though her mouth said no, her face said it was a lie. I could almost taste the nervous energy in the air as it buzzed between us.

"Then how do I make you feel?"

She sucked in a breath and straightened her back. "That's irrelevant, Chase. We're here to discuss *you*. Let's not get sidetracked, okay?"

"See, we can't get sidetracked, Glory, because right now, we're on two different tracks headed in opposite directions. I don't tell my secrets to strangers."

"And how do you suggest we fix that, Chase?"

"You answer my questions, and I'll answer yours. Do we have a deal?"

"That's not how *this* works." She motioned between the two of us.

"Well, I'm 'different from the others'. You said it yourself. But I can't help but wonder how different, and *why*? So again, do we have a deal?"

Her eyes locked on mine and she dropped her voice. "Deal." Her hushed tone was unnecessary. No one could hear us from where my cell was. We were down the hall at the opposite end of the guard station. And if there was one thing I knew about V.D., it was that he was a lazy prick any time he could get away with it.

"So, I'll ask you again. Do I make you nervous?"

She sucked her lower lip into her mouth and ran her teeth over it, popping it back out. "A little, yes."

"Why? Are you scared of me?"

She shook her head. "No, I'm not scared. If I'm being

honest, I'm intrigued. You're an interesting guy to me, Chase."

"That's no reason to be nervous. Unless…" I paused. "Unless it's how I make you feel that worries you."

She pulled out her notebook and crossed her leg to rest it on. "You got your question. It's my turn."

It was too fucking cute when she tried to get all bossy with me.

"Go on, shoot."

"What happened the other day, Chase? Why are you in the hole?"

Fuck.

I should have seen that one coming, but didn't.

"Uh, right, well…" I could either tell her the full truth or conceal some of it. But I figured she needed the warning to stay away from Stubbles, so I told her everything. Apart from the bit about him calling her my girlfriend. Or him accusing me of white knighting. "So yeah, I hit him. But again, he had it coming. He's a fucking creep, and you'd better stay away from him."

"Warden Johns isn't allowing him to return to the group."

"Good. I'm glad."

"But why did you stand up for me, Chase? You threw away your parole hearing, and you don't know me."

Because you're mine.

Because if anyone's going to defile you, it'll be me, and I'll fuck up any guy who thinks otherwise.

"You're around my sister's age. I guess I'm just used to defending women from the creeps who try to harm them."

She frowned. "I remind you of your sister?" The disappointment in her tone was evident.

"No Gloria, you do not remind me of my sister. The

thoughts I have of you are anything but sisterly, believe me."

"You think of me?"

"Don't you think of me? Your turn is over, by the way. It was a long one, so you owe me a few."

We talked until the hour was almost done. I learned she grew up in Albuquerque, New Mexico. That her parents still lived there. I learned she was twenty-six, only a year older than my sister, Liberty, which meant that there were eight years between us. That she had one older sister, and she was a 'real' doctor, unlike Gloria, according to her parents. Her sister was a surgeon, just like their father.

"It's been good talking to you, Chase. I'm not sure how much you benefited from this, but maybe you should be the one offering therapy. Because I feel great," she laughed, and the sound made my cock stir.

"As long as it's you I'm talking to, I'll always benefit."

Her smile faded, and she shuffled in her seat. There were those nerves again. She'd relaxed during our conversation, but I guess I caught her off-guard.

"Which leaves me with my homework for you." She pulled a pen and a few loose sheets of paper from her bag, and stood, crossed the room, and set them on my pillow. "I want you to make a list of things you're grateful for. We'll discuss them on Thursday."

"They won't let me keep those."

"Oh." She picked it back up and shoved it between the bedframe and the mattress. "What they don't know won't hurt them."

She turned to head to the door, and I followed. "Hey, doc. I have some homework for you, too." She spun to face me and took a step back. "What is it?"

I took another step toward her until I was close enough I could have kissed her. I silently cursed at the handcuffs on my wrists. Without them, I would've just grabbed her and pulled her to me. But my words would have to do what my hands could not. "Hey Doc, the next time you're thinking of me. If you get any urges…"

"What urges?"

"The kind where you touch yourself."

Her lips formed an 'o' as she sucked in a rattled breath. "Chase—that's not appropriate."

"What they don't know won't hurt them, right? Besides, that's the real reason I make you nervous, isn't it? I make you nervous because you're feeling the same way I do. You want me just as much as I want you. But unlike me, you've got a lot to lose. I'd be fucking nervous too if I were you."

Her eyebrows raised as her eyes went wide, but there was a longing in them.

Screw it.

I pressed a soft kiss to her lips, dragging her bottom lip between my teeth, and she placed her hand on my chest, but didn't push me away. I backed her to the wall, kissing her harder, my tongue exploring her mouth. She let out a soft moan that traveled all the way to my cock. I wanted to touch her. I tilted my head to the side, kissing her neck as she wrapped her arms around mine.

"They—they're going to come for me any minute now. We can't get caught like this."

I didn't want to stop, but she was right. Footsteps sounded in the hall and I heard the jangle of the keys Davis kept on his belt.

I groaned, stepped back from her, and returned to sit on the bed. "Consider that a little inspiration for you while you complete your assignment. I want a full *oral* report next time."

The cell door clicked open before she had the chance to reply, and good old V.D. stepped in. "Ready to go?"

Gloria nodded and hurried out of the room. "See you Thursday, Mr. Franklin."

I turned my back to her so Victor could remove the cuffs. Once free, I rubbed at my wrists.

"See you soon, Doc."

Chapter Six

Gloria

I sat down on the sofa in my apartment. Thoughts of Chase and his assignment were at the forefront of my mind. What did he mean by a full oral report?

My stomach flipped when I realized he might have been asking for me to do more than just tell him what I'd thought about or done.

When Warden Johns said she was going to assign trustworthy guards to the unit, I didn't think Victor would be among them. But he was a bit of a kiss-ass at work. I guess she didn't know the real him as I did. Victor Davis was the furthest thing she could get from trustworthy.

And the handcuff thing, I guess I should have been relieved by it, and if it was anyone else, I would have been. I clenched my jaw and huffed. But it was Chase's hands that were bound. And I'd never wanted to be touched more by a man in my entire life than I did him.

I tucked my legs beneath me, took my laptop off the side table, opened up a search engine, and started typing.

'How to pick handcuffs.' I hovered over the search and paused.

I backspaced, deleting it all.

Had I gone insane?

How many rules was I willing to break for Chase Franklin?

I knew how many I wanted to break. All of them. But there's a divide between what one wants to do and what one should do, and I needed to remember that.

I needed clarity, and I'd been in a state of arousal since I'd left him earlier that day, which wasn't doing me any favors. I set the computer back on the table and sighed. Thinking about how he'd backed me against the wall, how my skin tingled all over when he kissed me on the neck. Even hands-free, he knew how to drive me wild. Where would I have wanted him to touch me if he could have?

Everywhere.

But first, I'd have liked to feel his hand slip over my neck to hold me to our kiss with his other arm wrapped around me, pressing my body against his. I slid back into a reclined position on my couch, tucked my hand past the hem of my lounge shorts, and shut my eyes.

He smelled of soap, but the clean smell was intoxicating enough on its own. I dipped my fingers deeper within, pulling the wetness that pooled there up to my clit. The way his stubble tickled my skin when he teased me into a kiss.

I circled my clit with two fingers, imagining it was his hand instead of mine. That he was right there with me, his body warm against mine, as his hand explored between my legs. My pussy ached to know the feel of him—to be filled by him.

A hollow feeling overcame me, one that I knew only he could fill. Despite it, I persisted, doing my best to conjure up what it would feel like to have him buried deep within me, stretching me.

He was off-limits, but I couldn't have cared less at that moment. My fantasies were safer than acting on it in reality. Maybe they would be enough.

I sucked in a breath, feeling my release as it rose to the surface, and broke, right there, alone in my living room with a mind full of Chase.

Thwack. Thwack. Thwack.

Three hard knocks came from my door.

I ripped my hands from my pants and my heart hammered in my chest as the intimacy of the moment was stolen by the intrusion.

"Gloria." A chill ran over me. I knew that voice.

Axel.

More knocking. I hurried to the door and unlocked it. "What do you want?"

He pushed his way into the room, scanning it. "What? Just because we aren't together anymore doesn't mean I can't come to check up on you, does it?"

"I don't need checking up on, Axel." It'd been over two years since we had been together, if you could even call it that, since I'd been more like a pet or plaything than a girlfriend to him. But these visits were no less frequent than they had been when we first broke up.

He stroked his beard and crossed the room, flopping down on the sofa with his arms outstretched over the back. "That's not what I hear."

I wandered into the kitchen to wash my hands and poured a glass of water. "You shouldn't be hearing anything at all."

"If you didn't want to be watched, dollface, you

shouldn't have taken a job at the prison. You know I've got eyes and ears all over that place. What are you up to there, anyhow?"

"Doing my job."

"Right. About that. It seems my regular guy is sick. I'm going to need you to deliver something for me this week. You'll do that for me, won't you, babe?"

I leaned against the counter, setting my glass next to me. I would have offered him something, but I had no desire for him to stick around. "No, I won't. Listen, I let you in because we need to talk. These surprise visits need to stop. This will be the last time you visit me. Am I making myself clear?"

He leaned his head back on the wall and let out a deep chuckle. "You know, it's strange. I rescued a girl from her shitty family. Her parents wouldn't let her go to the university program of her choosing. But *I* made it happen. And once she was done, guess what? She split. You'd think that maybe she'd given me a bit more loyalty in return." He turned his head to look at me, his light eyes piercing through the dim living room. "Wouldn't you think?"

"I appreciate everything you did for me, Axel. I do. But you know as well as I do why we split up. We weren't looking for the same things. And your lifestyle, well, it's just not what I need to be tied up with."

"It was good enough for you when you were twenty. My money was good enough for you."

"Well, sometimes the person you pick at twenty isn't the person you would pick when you're older. I'm sorry if that hurts you."

He waved a hand at me. "I'm not hurt, babe. I'm impatient." He sat forward, picking up the novel I had on the table and flipping it over before tossing it back. "Anyway, if you won't help me out, I gotta jet and find someone else who will."

He stood, hooking his thumbs in his belt loops, faced me, and said, "I'll give you some space. Since you're insisting on it." He headed for the door and opened it. "But, Gloria," He looked over at me. "Don't make me wait too much longer. Your time is already up." With that, he stepped into the hall and pulled the door closed behind him.

I knew what I should have done. Run. Put as much distance between me and Axel as I could. Start fresh. But I wasn't sure he wouldn't follow me, besides I'd worked hard to build the life I had. Going to the police wasn't an option. He'd bragged more times than I could count about how deep he had them in his pocket. They weren't any better off than I was.

But he couldn't take credit for everything.

I regretted taking his money, but our relationship had been a genuine one. Sure, he financed some of my education, but I had scholarships, and I'd worked hard too.

And then there was my work at the prison, with Chase in particular. I couldn't just leave that all behind. I stood to lose so much by leaving. But every time Axel came by, he made it clear I was on borrowed time. That I might lose so much more by staying put.

My laptop beckoned me back to the sofa, and I continued the search I'd abandoned earlier.

I didn't know how much time Chase and I would have together, given our respective situations.

We needed to make the most of it.

Chapter Seven

Chase

"This should be working. The guy in the video did it exactly like this," Gloria said as she fumbled with the paperclip in her hand. Twisting it around in the keyhole of the handcuffs.

At least Victor was out sick and the guard today had the decency to cuff my hands at the front instead of behind me. It was a lot more comfortable.

"You're awfully eager to have my hands loose, Doc. Any reason why?"

She looked at me, from where she was kneeling in front of me on the floor, the blush rising in her cheeks. My mind turned dirty in an instant. She dropped her hands. "Sorry, I—"

I smirked at her. "I didn't say stop. I just wanted to hear you say it. You want my hands free because…" I prompted her to finish my sentence.

She sighed, rising to her feet with her pussy at my eye-level just behind her skirt. "It doesn't matter. I can't seem to do it."

"You're right, it doesn't. You know, they haven't cuffed my cock, right?"

She sucked in a sharp breath. "That's true."

"Come closer and hike your skirt up for me. I want to grade your homework."

She did as I asked, showing me her black lacy panties. "Those are pretty, baby girl, but that's not what I want to see."

She bit her lip and slipped her panties off, revealing her bare pussy to me.

I leaned forward and turned my ear to it. "What's that?" I pretended I was trying to listen to it. "A c minus? Really? That's too bad." I sat back. "You have some explaining to do, young lady. You aren't going to make the Dean's list with grades like that."

She bit back a laugh and forced a pout, pretending to be disappointed with the news of her poor grade. "Is there any extra credit I could do to make up for it?"

My cock rose to attention at her willingness to play along. Fuck, I hadn't doubted that she was the perfect woman, but that proved it. "Show me what you did."

"You—you want me to touch myself in front of you?"

"Well, of course, how am I going to help you improve without an example of your work?"

"You're a filthy man, Mr. Franklin," she said with a smile.

"Touch it, Gloria," I growled.

She slid her hand over the hood and dipped her fingers between them, sliding down, then back up to draw wetness to her clit. I fucking wanted at it myself, but I couldn't complain about a show.

"Good girl." I leaned forward. "I want to feel how wet you are. Would you like that?"

She nodded.

"Say it. Tell me you want it, baby."

Her voice was quiet. "I want you to touch me, Chase."

I crooked my finger and brushed the smooth skin of her thick thigh with it. "How bad do you want it?"

"Really bad. That's all I could think about."

"Me touching you?"

"Yes, and you inside me."

"Mmm, fuck, you know how to drive me wild. Spread your legs a bit more." She did, and I lifted my hands between them and turned the one, found her hole, and plunged two fingers deep inside her. She moaned at the sudden penetration. "Like that?" I hooked my fingers to stimulate her g-spot.

She let out a pant. "Oh my—wow, that feels incredible."

A gush of wetness released from her onto my hand. "Fuck, you're so wet. I want to taste it."

I pulled back to lie on my bed. "Come here. Sit on my face."

She took a tentative step forward. "I'll smother you."

"And if I die, I die. Now come sit on my fucking face, Glory, let's show that pussy of yours what an A-plus job feels like."

"You're crazy."

"No, I'm thirsty. Let me have a drink."

She just stood there, staring at me.

"Is this too much for you today?"

"No, but—"

"Well, the clock's fucking ticking. I want to feel you come on my face, Doc."

She kneeled on the bed and I slid down a little more so

she wouldn't be face-planted against the wall and she hiked her leg over me. "You're sure about this?"

Fuck, I wish my hands were free. I would have grabbed her full, meaty hips and pulled her right down on me. "Yes, I'm sure. Sit down."

She braced herself by placing one hand on the wall and lowered herself down on me. I groaned as her wetness spread over my lips. Tilting my chin, I found her clit and circled it with my tongue until her body shivered.

I lapped at her slowly at first, but when I picked up the pace, her hips were bucking involuntarily as she full-on rode my face.

My cock was harder than I'd remembered it being in years, my balls tight and full, aching for release.

Her moans were becoming more frequent. I sucked at her clit and she tensed up her thighs, squeezing my face in place. I flicked at her a few more times and she released on my tongue. She climbed off of me and collapsed onto the bed next to me. I wished my arms were free to hold her.

"How much time do we have left?"

She looked at her watch. "Ten minutes."

"Then I'm going to have to make this quick." I sat up. "Help me out here." I looked down at my jumpsuit. She hurriedly undid the buttons and pulled it down, reached into it, freeing my cock.

There was no time to focus on how good it felt to be touched by her for the first time. I wanted inside her.

Right. Fucking. Now.

"Get on your elbows and knees. I want your ass high." She flipped over and stuck her luscious ass in the air. I bent forward and bit it and she yelped.

"Quiet baby, if you're going to be loud, use the pillow."

I shuffled closer and lifted my arms, placing my hands on the small of her back, and turned my wrists to hold her as best as I could manage. I pressed my hard cock against her as she circled her hips to help guide me. As soon as we were lined up, I rocked into her and her face turned into the pillow to try to muffle her loud cry.

Fuck, I hope they hadn't heard that.

I slammed in and out of her fast and hard. We didn't have much time, but I wanted to release inside her. To fill her quivering pussy to the brim with my hot seed. "How does it feel having me inside you?"

"Full."

"How'd you like to get fuller?"

"How?"

I slowed my thrusts because I was getting close. "I want to come in you." A tingle ran up my spine. Slowing down wasn't helping. She'd better hurry up and answer or it was going to be too late. At this rate, I wasn't even sure I could pull out without accidentally spilling into her.

She grabbed my pillow and, before burying her face in it, said, "Do it."

There was no time to waste. I slammed in and out of her as hard and fast as I could, her moans muffled by the pillow. I groaned, shooting spurt after spurt of my cum straight into her. I collapsed back onto my heels.

She quickly sat up and fixed my clothing. I pressed my lips against hers, kissing her deeply. She hopped up, slipped her panties back on, and fixed her skirt.

When her butt hit her chair, she exhaled in relief that we hadn't been caught. We locked eyes, smiling at each other from across the room.

Except I had a little more to smile about, knowing that she'd be leaving there with a pussy full of my cum. I licked my lips. But I guess she'd left her mark too. I could still taste her on me.

I rolled my shoulders. They felt loose, like years of

tension that I didn't know I'd been carrying had disap-peared. "If I'd known this was what therapy would be like, I'd have signed up for it years ago."

She laughed. "What can I say? I'm good at my job, Chase."

Chapter Eight

Gloria

The remainder of Chase's time spent in solitary flew by. We'd decided to not waste time trying to pick the handcuffs like we had that second visit.

I still didn't know what it would feel like to have him touch me in the way I knew he wanted to, nor had we seen each other stark naked, but I was thankful for what we had shared.

But there was a nagging part of me that couldn't help but wonder how he would react when he saw me naked. Would he like what he saw? It was easy to feel secure without every lump and bump exposed.

We had our visits down to a fine science. Sex first, then instead of cutting it close like we had that first time, we spent the rest of the time talking.

He told me about losing his mother, how protective he'd become of his sister, Liberty, and how he regretted keeping her from being with his best friend, Nico. Because if he hadn't, she wouldn't have ended up with her ex-husband. And if she'd never been with Paul, then Chase would have never ended up in jail.

He'd opened up about so many things once I stopped trying to be his therapist and somewhere along the line, it'd become clear I was his girlfriend. The time always flew by when we were alone together.

But everything was about to change.

We'd no longer have the privacy of his isolation room. We were back to meeting in the same room where we'd first met for the anger management group.

They added a table for one-on-one sessions and I'd picked up a couple of other inmates for them to cover our tracks. I didn't want Chase's special treatment to become too obvious, after all. We'd just have to endure this until his release when we could be together.

Chase sat down at the table as the other guys left the room. I'd chosen to meet with him last to reduce the risk of other inmates arriving early for their appointments and interrupting us.

We wouldn't be able to do much, but the way Chase looked at me spoke volumes, and I didn't want anyone else seeing it.

Chase rubbed at his stubble. "How was your weekend, Doc?"

I smiled at him before I glanced over at Victor, who stood by the door. It was only the three of us left in the room. "Uneventful. You look tired, Mr. Franklin. Is every-thing all right?" The formalities felt so awkward and forced now.

"It's noisy back in gen pop and it's been keeping me up at night. I just need to get used to it again. Not to mention..." He smirked, and I knew he was champing at the bit to mention our extra-curricular activities. Men always seemed to sleep better when they were getting regular sex.

"Not to mention is right," I said with a laugh. His smile grew wider, revealing his deep dimple, and he swiped his hand over his face to regain his composure.

My heart leaped anytime he showed his dimple. He was all man, but in those moments, I could see the mischievous boy that still lived somewhere within him.

I'd never felt about anyone the way Chase Franklin made me feel. We'd only known each other a short time, but it was becoming too obvious that I was falling deep, if I hadn't already fallen head over heels, in love with him.

Victor approached the table. "I'm going to go grab a coffee, do you want one, Gloria?" They'd taken away our right to have coffee at the meetings after one inmate threw his in the face of another one the week before. "No, I'm good. Thanks for the offer, though."

As soon as he left the room, Chase lunged forward with his free hands, slipping his hand around the side of my neck and pulling me to him for a kiss. He pressed his forehead to mine. "Fuck, Glory, I've waited forever to do that." He pressed his lips to mine again. We wouldn't have long, but a few stolen kisses would have to do.

"Oh, I forg—what the fuck?"

Chase and I both snapped back. Victor stood frozen in place with the cuffs dangling in front of him.

I dropped my head down. My heart was hammering in my chest and my breathing was rapid. My fight-or-flight instinct had kicked in hard. But there was nowhere to go and nothing that could be done.

Victor had come back to cuff Chase, of course he had. And that was it. He'd caught us.

It was over.

Victor crossed the room, cuffing Chase. "I'll be back with Warden Johns. You two are going to have a lot of explaining to do."

He hurried out of the room.

"Doc, chin up," Chase said.

But I couldn't. I didn't want to face the warden. She'd trusted me and I'd abused that trust.

"Look at me right now, Glory."

I did as I was told and met his gaze.

"Gloria, I'm sorry, but I need you to know something before they get back. I love you."

My heart ached, but I mustered a smile. I'd wanted to hear those words come from him, more than anything, but I'd hoped it would be under better circumstances. "I love you too, Chase. But—uh—I'm going to leave Arizona. That guard…"

"Davis?"

I nodded. "He's bad news. He knows my ex and once he tells him what happened here today, it won't be good for either of us. The best thing I can do for us is to get out of town. Maybe he'll be too distracted by my disappearance to come after you. Once I'm settled, I'll write to you, okay?"

"You need to go to the police."

"It's pointless. He's the president of the Desert Demons motorcycle club, and he's got the police wrapped around his finger. Just trust me. I need to do this."

"Fuck!" Chase slammed his fist on the table and I jumped. "I wish I could go with you, Glory. I'm a fucking idiot for putting you in this position when I can't protect you from the fall out. Why didn't you tell me about your ex?"

I sighed. "I didn't want to spoil our time together. But now it's too late."

"Promise me something?" His eyes were wide with hope.

"Anything."

"That you'll stay safe. Get as far away from here as you can. Don't worry about me. I can handle myself. But promise me…" He paused. "That this won't be the end of us? That you'll wait for me?"

Warden Johns and Victor entered the room just as I whispered, "I promise."

Victor hauled Chase off, and the warden folded her arms with a sigh. "Grab your things, Doctor Moore. We need to talk."

Chapter Nine

Chase

Three Months Later

"Franklin, you have a letter." I stood from the table in the common area and made my way over to the guard.

It had to be from Gloria.

Liberty, my sister, only came to visit or I called her and there was no one else to write to me. Luc followed as I returned to our cell and tore open the envelope.

Chase,

I'm sorry it took so long for me to write. But I needed to wait until the dust settled. You don't know how much I've missed you and it's been an agonizing wait. I'm safe in New Mexico now.

The postmark confirmed she was in Albuquerque. She'd gone home. She should've gone somewhere no one would think to look for her, but at least she was around her family. Maybe they were more accepting of her than they had been in the past.

My new job keeps me busy, but it's going well. I won't go into too many details about it for obvious reasons, but I want you to know that despite everything, I'm okay. There's extra money on your account so you can call me, and I hope to hear from you soon.

The letter was brief, but she gave me her phone number and signed it with love, leaving her name off.

"Well?" Luc gave my shoulder a shove.

I nodded. "She gave me her number."

"Shit, it's about damn time. Your moping around was getting tiring."

"I wasn't moping around. I was worried. It's fucking awful being cut out and trapped in here."

"Well, what are you waiting for? Go call her."

"It's the middle of the day. She'd be at work. I'll wait until later."

"Oh yeah, good thinking. I'm nervous, man."

"About your parole hearing?"

"Yeah. But it's more than that. I've got nothing once I get out of here. My girl left me when I caught charges. I'm going to be starting over. Shit, I'm moving in with my grandmother. I'm a forty-year-old man that'll be living with his grandmother. How fucking pathetic is that?"

"You'll figure it all out once you're free. Besides, you've got me now."

He laughed. "You know you're a sappy bastard now that you're in love."

"Nah, you've kept me sane in here. I owe you one."

"Well, you've driven me nuts," he said with a cackle. "But I appreciate you."

In a few days, Lucian would be up for parole, and he'd get it for sure. He didn't belong in jail anymore than I did. Soon, I'd be alone. I patted my pocket with the letter inside, reminding myself that wasn't true.

Gloria was back.

<hr>

I picked up the phone, stated my name, and waited for the automated system to do its thing.

"Hello?"

"Hey, baby."

"Who is this?" she asked.

"It's Chase. Gloria?"

"You've got to be kidding me." I heard the phone rustling and the murmur of two women talking.

"Leave me be," Gloria said before she spoke into the receiver. "Chase?"

"Yes, who was that? You sound alike."

"My sister," she sighed. "It's so good to hear from you. How are you doing?"

"Much better now that I've heard your voice."

She was quiet for a moment, but I could almost hear the smile on her face when she said, "I've missed you so much."

"I've missed you too, Glowbug."

She laughed before I could hear her hand cover the

receiver and the sound of murmured voices. "Sorry about that. Glowbug? What's that? When did you come up with that?"

"Just now. It was a toy I had when I was a kid. But it fits you, I think. Because I want to hold you so fucking bad and you light up my world. You seem busy. Did you want me to call another time?"

"No, no, please don't go. Has Mr. Control himself gone soft for me?"

There was an attempt at a playful tone to mask the pleading in her voice. I could tell the months had worn on her. But she was safe and well and I was glad for it. We'd make up for the lost time. "You know I'll always be hard for you when you need me to be. You missed me, didn't you, baby?"

"I did. I thought about you every day, multiple times a day."

"Oh, you did, did you?" I dropped my voice low. "And what did you think about, *exactly*?"

She giggled, "I know that tone, Chase. What if someone hears you?" I smiled, happy that I could break some of the tension to get her sounding more like herself.

I chuckled. "There's no one close by, and besides, it isn't me that's about to get noisy."

"Oh, really?"

"Yes, I miss hearing you moan for me, Glory. It's been way too fucking long. What are you wearing?"

"Pajamas."

"It's six p.m."

"I change as soon as I get home because I like to be comfy. Is that a crime?"

"You bet it is. Any clothing on you is criminal. If I were there, you'd be wearing nothing at all most days. Touch yourself for me?"

"Hold on," I heard the phone rustle and the creak of a door before it clicked closed.

"Are you getting comfortable?"

"I am."

"So tell me, baby. Are you wet for me?"

"I'm always wet for you, Chase."

I groaned, wishing I could feel her slick heat first hand. "Take two fingers and dip them inside for me. Pretend it's my hard cock filling your pussy."

A guy approached the phone wall, I flashed him a glare, and he doubled back. He was a new guy in the unit and I wasn't one to be a dick, but I wanted the privacy. I turned my body and leaned over the phone with my back to the room and dropped my voice. "Are you doing it?"

"I am."

"And how does it feel?"

"Good, but I wish it was you."

"It will be soon. But I need you to keep that pussy happy for me in the meantime. No more failing grades, understand me?"

"I do." Her voice was breathy, and I could tell she was doing as I asked.

"Good girl. But I want to hear it. Can you get noisy for me?"

She moaned into the phone and my cock twitched in my jumpsuit. I'd have to stay calm but commit the sound of her to memory for later.

"That's it, good job. I'd fill that sweet cunt of yours so full with my cum. Would you like that?"

"I would."

"Good, because once I'm out of here, there'll be no stopping me. I'll fuck you, fill you, and fuck you again. Because you're mine, Gloria. All fucking mine."

She let out a whimper of a moan. "I'm all yours, Chase."

"Always?"

"Always, I—" she moaned louder, and I dropped my head down to make sure my growing erection wasn't too obvious. I took a deep breath, trying to calm myself.

Fuck, she sounded as beautiful as she was.

"When I get my hands on you again, you'll be the one going hands free. I'm going to tie you up and have my way with you. For as long as I want and in whatever way I choose. How does that sound?"

She didn't respond. At least not with words, but I could hear her breath quicken as her moans grew more frequent.

"Oh baby, I know that sound. You want to come for me, don't you?"

She let out a desperate whimper. "I do."

"Fuck yes, do it then. Let me know how good it feels."

As if on command, she broke. Her cries of ecstasy filled my ear. I imagined she was coming undone around my cock and it throbbed with need.

I took another deep breath to calm myself. A shower might be in order after this. But in the meantime, I didn't need to be popping a rock solid erection right in the middle of the unit.

As her orgasm subsided, I let out a satisfied hum. "Thank you. That was the most beautiful thing I've heard in a while."

"Wagon up!" someone called out behind me, to alert everyone that it was meal time again.

"What was that?"

"It's dinner time. That's all."

"You should go eat."

"I don't want to go yet."

I wasn't ready to let her go. It took us three months to get to this point, and I didn't want the call to end so soon.

"Go eat. You can call me later if you get the chance. Or tomorrow. I expect to hear from you daily."

"Of course, I'll call every day my Glowbug."

"I love you, Chase."

"I love you too, Gloria."

She sighed, like hanging up was the last thing she wanted to do. "Okay, go now. I'm not good at goodbyes. At least not when you're involved."

My woman was too fucking sweet for words sometimes. "All right, if I can't call you back. Good night and sleep well, baby."

"Night." She made a kissing noise into the phone and I smiled before hanging up.

I stood by the phone for a minute after, happy that she'd kept her promise to me. That, after waiting and wondering for three months, she was still my girl.

It was going to be a slow race to the finish for us. I still had a good chunk of time left to serve. But we had each other again, and I felt confident we'd make it to the finish line—together.

Chapter Ten

Gloria

Eight Months Later

Chase and I continued our love affair over the phone. While some months passed faster than others, our devotion to one another never wavered.

It was the day of his parole hearing, and while I didn't see why they wouldn't grant it to him, the worry was still there that we might have to wait another six months until he was free. I was eager for his release, but prepared for any outcome.

Or so I thought…

A rap sounded on my apartment door and I looked around the apartment for my purse to pay the delivery driver for the food I ordered. "Coming!"

My job working supervision for a crisis hotline wasn't

glamorous, and we were short staffed so I'd been working long hours. Takeout had become a way of life, but I was thankful, all things considered, to be employed at all.

The warden was more concerned with preserving her delicate reputation than destroying mine when she'd learned of Chase and me. She didn't want the word getting around that she'd allowed unsupervised access to an inmate in isolation, so she swept the whole incident under the rug. The only condition was that I resign from my position, which I did.

I hurried into the bedroom and found my purse on the bedside table where I'd taken it when I changed into loungewear. I'd picked a skimpy pair of shorts and a lacy camisole.

Even though Chase wouldn't be able to see me, he'd be asking me, and I wanted to celebrate the occasion with something more provocative than my usual pajama pants and oversized t-shirt.

I'd left the Tucson area the same day they'd discovered Chase and me. With only one packed bag in my trunk, I abandoned my apartment with furnishings intact before driving the six hours to Albuquerque. I needed to put as much distance between Axel and me as I could before the word got back to him.

My sister let me move in with her when I first arrived and we lived together for another month after Chase and I began talking again. Her judgment about the situation wasn't fierce, but every time the phone rang, I felt it. She'd just have to meet him for herself to see that he wasn't just your typical inmate.

I crossed the room, wallet in hand, fishing out enough cash to cover the food and tip before unlocking the door and twisting the knob.

Before I even got the door open, it threw me back into

the opposing wall. A gush of air forced out of my lungs. I slid down to the floor, my lungs clawing to refill as I looked up at the figure hovering over me.

Axel.

He grabbed my upper arms and pulled me to my feet. "Time's up, dollface."

He half-dragged me to the couch as my feet struggled to keep up with his pace in my startled, oxygen-deprived state.

Axel stood over me, pacing back and forth. "You ran. Fuck. After everything I did for you, you fucking ran. And to Albuquerque, of all places? This is the last place I thought you'd come back to, Gloria. The way you left your apartment, I thought you'd been fucking murdered or something."

My breathing regulated. "Why didn't you call the cops then?" I was goading him. Because I knew why he hadn't called them. People like him didn't involve cops.

"That's not how I roll. But now I know the truth." He reached into his jacket pocket and tossed a handful of envelopes at me.

They were mine.

I gathered the few letters I'd addressed to Chase. A chill ran through me.

"Where did you get those? Victor?"

"Victor betrayed me almost as bad as you. He's being dealt with as we speak. He never told me about your incident at the prison. Seems the warden promised him some promotion," he sighed. "Fuck, I can't count on anyone but myself these days." He sat perched on my coffee table and smacked his hands down on my knees. "I figured he was two-timing me, so I branched out. My new guy found out that a Chase Franklin might interest me. It seems Victor wasn't beyond taking the spoils from both sides. But this new guy, damn, he's good, one 'routine' inspection later and guess what he found?" He flicked at the stack of envelopes in my hand. "I should've known you'd be whoring around on me." He hooked his finger behind the strap of my camisole and ran it down. I wished I had worn my usual pajamas. "Because that's you, isn't it, dollface? You don't have a fucking loyal bone in your sexy body, do you?" He stared at me and waited for my reply.

I was too afraid to speak.

Anything I wanted to say wouldn't please him, and I worried about the consequences Chase might face. I crossed my arms across my chest, crumpling the letters as I did.

"Well, I guess I'll answer for you. You don't. First, you rebelled against your parents with me. Then you used me. And now you've rebelled against me with a fucking convict. Talk about picking low-hanging fruit. Fuck, Gloria, we almost had it all."

"We had nothing." I looked down at the envelopes clutched to my chest and swallowed hard, hoping that Chase hadn't already suffered for the discovery of them.

Axel grabbed my chin, forcing me to look up at him. "Who's fault is that?"

"No one's. Life's like that sometimes."

"Wrong," he sneered. "You have no fucking clue how wrong you are. The one at fault is staring back at you every time you look in a mirror." He ran his thumb over my mouth and pressed his lips to mine.

I clamped my lips tight and grit my teeth, my skin crawling from his touch. When he pulled back, a tear had forced out of one of my squinted eyes and ran down my cheek.

He swiped it away and shook his head. "You're as stubborn as always. Doesn't matter. I'll fix your mess and you'll come around. So I hear lover boy's about to be released. He's bound to come for you, don't you think?" He smirked. "Except I'll be the one waiting for him."

"You can't do this."

He picked up my phone from the table and tossed it at me. "I sure can. Now call anyone who might expect you. Work, family, even friends. Anyone who might come for you and let them know you're sick and tell them not to come around."

I lifted the phone.

"And Gloria, don't fuck me around, or Franklin gets it. One call and he won't live long enough to see his freedom."

I paused with my finger over my sister's number. "If you can do that, why haven't you already?"

"Because he stole from me. It's personal. Besides, you need to see this. Once you see us go toe-to-toe, you'll realize who the better man is. But if you want to fuck around, I'll cut corners, and I don't think you'll like that much. So, be a doll and do as you're told."

And I did. I did everything he asked of me.

I wanted to warn Chase. To tell him not to come. I even tried to negotiate with Axel by telling him I'd break up with Chase. That I'd have nothing to do with him again if he let him go unharmed. But Axel wouldn't allow any of it.

And where did my negotiations get me?

Bound, gagged, and waiting for the worst in my living room.

Chapter Eleven

Chase

I sat outside the prison waiting for my sister, Liberty, and her husband, Nico, to arrive. Gloria hadn't picked up any of my calls for the past couple of days.

Liberty hopped out as soon as the car was in park and rushed to me, throwing her arms around me. I knew she carried a lot of guilt for what had happened and was eager to see me released.

Nico stood back for a few and then sauntered forward, giving me a pat on the back. "How's it feel to be a free man?"

I glanced over at Liberty. "Great, but I need a favor."

Nico nodded at me. "Shoot."

"I'll pay you back once I can get on my feet, but I need a loan."

Liberty shook her head at me. "You're staying with us.

I insist." I knew she was looking forward to me being around for a bit and I felt bad for letting her down, but I couldn't shake the feeling that Gloria was in some kind of danger.

The guard had confiscated all of my letters from her earlier that week. It wasn't V.D., but I didn't trust any of those fuckers.

I frowned, looking back at the prison behind me before sucking in a deep breath of fresh air. It was damn good to be on this side of the wall for a change. "I know, Libby, and I will, but I need to go to New Mexico for a couple of days."

She screwed up her face at me. "What for?" I tried to answer her, but she interrupted me before I had the chance. "Nevermind, you can't. You're on probation. You can't miss your appointment on Monday."

I ran my hand over my scalp and sighed. How could I make her understand? Finding Glory wasn't optional. "I know. But I have to find Gloria and make sure she's okay. She's—"

"Chase, please, just don't," Liberty begged.

Nico put his arm around her shoulders. "Let him continue, Lib."

I smiled at Nico. If there was one thing he understood, it was the need to do anything and everything to keep the woman that you love safe. "She's everything to me. You two have each other," I told Liberty before looking over at Nico. "Without her, my freedom means nothing. I'll explain everything later, I promise. But she needs me and I'm going to be there for her."

His eyes spoke to his sympathy, and he nodded. "Whatever you need is yours. Just don't come back empty-handed."

I stood tall and pushed my shoulders back, like a

soldier taking orders from his commanding officer. "I won't. Failure isn't an option."

I had Nico drop me off at Lucian's place. I needed wheels, and I didn't know what I was about to face in New Mexico. If anyone had my back, it would be Luc.

I thought about asking Nico, but we still hadn't had the chance to get reacquainted and I didn't know what we'd be walking into. If anything happened to him, it would crush Liberty and there was no way I could do that to her twice in a lifetime.

I stood on the stoop of the small a-frame house. He'd been living with his sick grandmother since his release. I knocked on the door and a few minutes later, a tiny old woman opened it. She smiled up at me. "May I help you, dear?"

"I'm sorry to bother you, ma'am but is Lucian home?"

"It's no bother, and you may be?"

"Chase Franklin."

"Oh, oh!" She waved her hand, ushering me into the house. "Lucian told me you were getting out." I stepped across the threshold. "You're much more handsome than I imagined from Lucian's stories."

"Thank you, ma'am. Your grandson has high standards of beauty."

She tutted. "Call me Glenora. And you've got that right, Chase. That boy, I love him, but he spends more time on his hair than I do on mine. But I suppose we love him still, don't we?"

I smiled at her. "That we do."

She clapped her hands. "Where are my manners? Have a seat. Would you like some sweet tea?"

Before I could answer, she hurried into the kitchen and I sat down on the sofa. Glenora's home was cozy, but dated. I wished I could've taken comfort in it, but there was only one thing on my mind as I sat there.

Gloria.

When Glenora returned with the iced tea in hand, I sat forward and took it from her while asking, "When are you expecting Luc?"

She looked over at the grandfather clock that stood in the living room's corner. "He should be home from work any minute now. He's late. Will you be staying for dinner?"

"I'll have to take a raincheck on that, but I'd love to some other time."

"You look burdened. Is everything all right?"

The door to her home swung open, and I turned to see Luc walk through the door and set his bag on the bench next to it. "Grandma, I'm ho—" He looked over at us seated in the living room. "Well, I'll be. Chase you fucker, it's good to see you."

"Lucian. Language," Glenora warned.

"Sorry, Grandma. Old habits."

He looked at me and tipped his head. I could tell by the way he was studying my face that he was no less perceptive about my distressed state than Glenora had been.

He sniffed the air. "Hey, Grandma, I think you should check on whatever you have in the oven."

She jumped from the chair. "My casserole!" she yelped, and hurried out of the room.

He moved into the living room and sat down across from me. "She's amazing, but she chars our meals most nights. Quick, give me the low down before she gets back."

"It's Gloria. I haven't heard from her in days."

"You think something is wrong?"

"I fucking *know* something is wrong. We were waiting

for the results of my parole hearing." I shook my head. "They took my letters. I think—shit, Luc—I think her ex may have found her. And it's all my fault."

"Fuck," he said, standing from his seat. "Let me grab a few things and we'll go."

"She's in Albuquerque."

"I don't care. If you think I'm letting you go alone, you're crazy. Who knows what you're walking into, Chase? You need me."

He was right on all accounts. We had no clue what we were walking into.

Chapter Twelve

Gloria

Music blared from the living room where Axel was piss drunk. He'd moved me to the bedroom and handcuffed me to one of the metal bedposts.

I could still smell his booze-soaked breath from earlier, when he'd muttered something about leaving me alone to 'think about what I'd done' and told me to call for him once I'd come to my senses about us.

The most he did was feed me and let me use the washroom. Apart from the forced kiss on the first day, he hadn't attempted anything else. How I got so lucky, I'll never know.

Then again, he was holding me hostage and waiting to ambush my boyfriend, so, maybe I wasn't too lucky.

There was a rap on the bedroom window. My heart leaped and pounded in my ears. I sat forward and the clank of metal on metal reminded me of my state. There was a crouched figure on the other side, motioning for me to let him in.

I squinted. He was too thin-framed to be Chase. Then again, I hadn't seen him in close to a year. Maybe he'd lost some muscle definition?

"I can't," I mouthed, pointing at my cuffed hand. He pulled at the window again. It felt strange to be relying on some unknown person for my potential rescue.

The door swung open and Axel came through it. The figure disappeared from view and I looked away. "I gotta piss. Have you had enough time to think yet?"

"I—I have," I said. "You're right, we're meant to be together. You can un-cuff me now."

He approached the bed, leaning toward me. "Is that so?"

I recoiled backward.

He laughed. "You're a fucking shitty liar, Gloria. Nice try, though. What kind of dumb-fuck do you take me for?"

My heart hammered in my chest. "You just surprised me, that's all."

He waved me off, stumbling into the bathroom. Once he was done, he went back to the living room.

I slumped back and looked over at the window, upset that I'd ruined my one chance. The figure reappeared. I had to do something.

But what?

Think, Gloria, think.

That's it!

I put up my hand, signaling for whoever it was to wait a minute. It must have been shock or stress, or that he'd threatened to have Chase harmed that had made me forget, but I had to get free.

I turned to my side, opened the bedside table drawer,

and felt around inside. There wouldn't be a paperclip, but I'd had little luck with those anyhow. My fingertip ran along the crinkled edge of a bobby pin, and I plucked it from the drawer and bit down on it before closing the drawer again.

Using my mouth and my free hand, I pried the prongs apart, and twisted the pin into what I hoped was the correct shape for the keyhole on the cuffs. I tried it. My nervous fingers fumbled, but it didn't matter. The loop I'd created was too narrow. I bit down on it again, prying it open and bent it into a wider loop this time. It fit. I turned it in the hole. What was it that the man in the video had said? How many turns?

Damn it.

It had been so long.

The music stopped, and I heard a knock at the front door. I glanced over at the man in the window. He was still there.

Waiting for you to get it together.

I took a deep breath, steadying my hand, and gave the hair pin a couple more turns. The handcuff fell open.

I did it!

I wanted to scream or jump for joy. But I rushed to the window and unlocked it, sliding it open. The man reached in, took my hand, and helped me out onto the fire escape.

I wrapped my arms around my chest, sheltering myself from the breeze. Axel hadn't let me change out of the outfit I'd been wearing the night he arrived. I felt gross and exhausted, but relieved to have some small bit of freedom.

I could see his face in the moonlight and it saddened me to see that, as I had suspected, it wasn't Chase. "Who are you?" I asked.

"Lucian," he said, keeping his voice low.

Lucian? As in Chase's Lucian? A chill ran through me.

The knock at the door.

It had to have been Chase. I wanted to go back inside, but when I turned for the window, Lucian stopped me.

"Stay here." He handed me a mobile phone. "Call the police. Chase wanted you out first, but I'll go help him now."

Lucian climbed through my window, crossed the room to my bedroom door, and paused with his back against the wall.

I woke up the phone in my hands to find it locked. After pressing the emergency option on the screen, I called and waited for someone to pick up.

"Hi, yes, I'd like to report a hostage situation."

The operator asked who was involved.

"Me, can you please hurry?" I croaked out. Unable to get my mind off Chase as I gave them my address.

A shot fired from within the apartment and I dropped to the metal grate of the fire escape, scraping my back against the brick wall, my heart thumping.

"Please hurry," I cried out. "Before it's too late."

Chapter Thirteen

Chase

I knocked on the door of Gloria's apartment, unsure of what I was walking into. My gut told me her ex would be inside. But would he be alone?

I'd sent Lucian up the fire escape. The building wasn't a big one, with only four apartments on each floor.

She lived in suite 404, which from a quick survey of the first floor, told me she'd be in the southeast corner of the building on the fourth floor.

The music from inside cut and I knocked again. A man with a long beard and a leather cut and jeans opened the door.

He chuckled, folding his arms across his chest and holding the door open with one booted foot. "We've been waiting for you."

We?

I glanced into the apartment. He appeared to be alone.

I clenched my jaw at the realization that he was referring to Gloria, *my* Gloria, when he said 'we'.

"Where is she?" I demanded, stepping forward into the suite. He didn't stop me.

There was a door which I assumed led to her bedroom and as I stepped toward it, I heard the click of a gun cocking. "Not so fast," he said. "You and I've got some talking to do first."

I pivoted on my heels to find myself staring down the barrel of his handgun. "Look, I'm not in the mood to chat. I came for my woman. That's it. Now, again, I'll ask you, where is she?"

He rushed forward. "Your woman? Your fucking woman?" he screamed in my face. I could smell the booze on his breath.

Big fucking mistake.

The gun was only inches from my chest. I smacked his arm and spun to the side, locking his arm in a hold. The gun fired, missing me, as I wrestled him to the ground, pulling it from his grip.

I leaned into him, using my weight to pin him to the floor. He was a big guy. I wouldn't be able to hold him for long as he squirmed and bucked against me.

I disarmed the gun, tossing the clip, sliding it under the couch, and making sure the chamber was clear before I tossed it to the other side of the room. I grabbed his shirt collar and pulled him up to a seated position with his help.

There was a confused look on his face before I bowed and head-butted him. He fell back unconscious.

The cops would be on their way. There was no way I was getting caught with a weapon in my hand since they had banned me from them. Besides, the only weapon I needed was my body. I rolled away from him, allowing my breath a moment to still.

A blood-curdling scream came from the bedroom. I scrambled to my feet and tried to push open the door, but something was in the way—or someone.

"Gloria, are you okay? Move whatever's by the door. Let me in."

"He's shot," she said between sobs. "The—the bullet. He was coming to help you. And—"

Ice rolled over my shoulders and crept up my neck. We shot Lucian? Fuck me.

"Deep breaths, baby. What's blocking the door?"

"His legs."

"Shift them. I just need enough room to get in there."

"There's so much blood," she said, her voice quivering.

I kept my hand on the door and, when I felt it go slack, I pushed my way in, scraping my body between the door and the frame.

Gloria was kneeling beside him. Lucian was still breathing, but she was right about the blood, there was *too* much of it.

I dropped to my knees, applying pressure to the wound with my bare hands. This isn't how things should have gone.

There was a bang on the front door.

"Come in," Gloria called out, hopping to her feet and squeezing through the door and into the living room to greet them.

"I'm sorry, Luc," I said, looking down at him, and he groaned. "This is all my fault."

The paramedics entered the room and took over, and I stepped back.

Gloria grabbed my arm and led me into the washroom.

I washed my hands and looked up in the mirror. Somehow, I'd ended up with Lucian's blood on my face. I must have touched it without realizing.

Gloria ordered me to have a seat on the toilet. She wet a face cloth, and with a gentle hand, patted it away. I looked up at her. It'd been months since I'd seen her in person. Once she was done with the cloth, she set it down and I hugged my arms around her waist, pulling her to me.

This wasn't how I imagined our reunion going—not even close. But her warm, soft midsection pressed against my face was everything I could have asked for at the moment.

I'd waited so long to have my arms wrapped around her. There had been so many nights when I'd lie awake in my cell thinking of her. Gloria changed me.

When I'd met her, I'd been a man with nothing, but with her in my life, I had more than I thought I ever would. More than I felt I deserved. I'd imagined our reunion so many times. How I planned to grab her and ravage her in the way I couldn't before. But there we were in her bathroom while my best friend bled out on her bedroom floor.

"I shouldn't have brought Lucian with me."

Gloria sighed, "You couldn't have known this would happen."

"Still, I shouldn't have. I let anger get the better of me. All I could focus on was the feeling that you were in danger, and I was seething inside. I only saw the risk to myself and that was a risk I'd take again—for you. But he didn't deserve this. And you didn't need to witness it. This —this proves what you've been telling me all along, Glow-bug. If I had a do-over, I wouldn't have charged in here. Sure, I knew I could take down Axel. I didn't even need to meet the guy to know that. But that didn't mean I should have. The way it went down…" I shook my head, remembering the brief struggle. "I might as well have pulled the trigger on Luc myself. That bullet was mine to take."

"Oh, Chase." She stroked my shaved head. I'd put my friend in a dangerous situation and who knew if he'd pull through or not? "You can't dwell on it now. The only thing you can do is take what you've learned here and apply it to future decisions."

She bent down and kissed me, and I pulled her onto my lap, deepening it. Her lips were salty from the tears she'd shed earlier. But her lips were like a balm for my soul, soothing me from the outside in.

"Ahem." I pulled back from our kiss to see a cop had poked his head around the corner. "We have a few questions."

Chapter Fourteen

Gloria

The police took Axel into custody to be charged with kidnapping and assault with a deadly weapon. After interviewing us, the police left. First responders had taken Lucian away.

The mood in my apartment was heavy as Chase's remorse permeated the air. He'd helped me clean up the mess that was left behind from Lucian's injury. Now he sat on my sofa with his gaze fixated on his hands like he expected blood to reappear on them.

"Come on, let's get cleaned up?" I told him.

He looked up at me and let out a deep sigh. "I don't deserve you, you know?"

I crossed the room and sat down beside him.

He continued, "Sure, I'm free now, but I can't offer you much else. You know that, right?"

I frowned. It broke my heart to see him in such

turmoil. "Chase, what happened here tonight is not your fault. My past decisions came back to haunt us. I've never met a more courageous and capable man than you, and I know in time you'll figure things out. If you think that what happened here tonight changes anything between us, you're wrong. We've been through so much, don't start doubting us now."

"I'm not. I love you, Gloria. Nothing can make me give up on us. I'm just stating facts and I need you to acknowledge the truth. I'm going to do everything in my power to be worthy of you—of your love. But this isn't how I pictured my release going, and while I gave that statement tonight, I half expected the police to haul me off right alongside Axel. Prison changed me in ways I didn't think it could. A part of me feels like I don't belong on the outside."

"That will fade in time. You've been out for less than a day and look at what you've gone through. How could you have any sense of normalcy yet? Please, babe, cut yourself some slack and allow yourself some time to adjust."

"My best friend got shot tonight, and it was my fault. What if I fuck up again and next time you're the one that gets hurt?"

"He'll pull through, Chase. I don't know how I know, but that's what my gut is telling me. You can't blame yourself. You're the best protector I've ever met. I've known that since the moment I first set eyes on you. How about we take a shower? We'll both feel better once we're cleaned up. In the morning, we'll visit Lucian, and you'll see. But for now, you need to unwind."

He looked over at me, his empty gaze replaced by the heated one he used to give me back when we'd carried on our secret love affair in the prison.

It was such a foreign feeling having him here. Having

him so close and yet not having his arms wrapped around me. This time was supposed to be our time, and Axel had robbed us of the reunion we'd both dreamed of for so long.

I was the one that should have been carrying the guilt that Chase was feeling over what had transpired. But that was the thing about Chase. He always carried the weight of the world on his shoulders. He took on other people's problems like he'd been the one to make the mistake. He'd done it with his sister and now with me.

When I'd first met him, I thought he'd used anger to exercise control over people. But now, I realized what he did was to try to regain control and give it back to those who couldn't seem to take it back for themselves. He never acted out on behalf of himself; it was always in the protection of others.

When I'd found that safe place with him, in that meeting room during our first therapy session, I knew from that very moment he'd become my protector. He proved it further when he'd thrown away his chance at freedom without a second thought, just to keep me out of harm's way.

And tonight, he proved that there was no boundary to the love he gave me. No fight too tough. There was no limit to the lengths he'd go to ensure I was safe.

Chase Franklin was a modern day knight in shining armor—*my* knight.

It was such a stark contrast to the love I was used to receiving that I should have been the one feeling unworthy. I should have been the one feeling flawed.

But I couldn't.

Not with Chase's dark eyes roaming over me the way they did. It wasn't just passion in them. There was appreciation. The entire universe was in my man's eyes at that moment, and I was in the very center of it all.

I leaned forward and gave him a soft kiss. It was my turn to take care of the man that had taken care of me since the day we met. I took his hand in mine and stood. He followed suit, and I led him to the bathroom.

While I ran the water to get it up to temperature, his arm slipped around my waist, hugging me from behind. He pulled my hair away from my neck and coated it in kisses.

"Fuck, you feel so good in my arms, baby." I could feel his erection pressing against my behind.

My pussy throbbed at the memory of being filled by him. The ache to become intimate with him again overcame me.

The arm that was wrapped around me slipped beneath my shirt and made its ascent to my breast, cradling my bare flesh in his hand and kneading it.

I leaned my head back on his chest, enjoying the feel of his warm palm against my skin.

He dropped his other hand to the waistband of my shorts and slipped his fingers behind it.

The steam from the shower filled the room as his fingers found their way between my folds, massaging my clit.

I moaned, tipping my head forward away from his chest to look at the falling water. "Chase, I need to shower first. And the water is going to run cold if we don't get in there soon."

He groaned, slipping his hand over my throat and tipping my head back again. "Do you think I care if you're a little dirty? You're going to be filthy by the time I'm done with you. I've waited so long to feel you. To get you naked."

My skin tingled, but not with pleasure. He had reminded me he hadn't seen me naked yet. Would my dimpled skin turn him off? I'd gained a bit more weight from all the takeout food since starting my new job. I regretted suggesting the shower at all.

He slipped his hands from my shorts and pulled them down, and they fell the rest of the way to the floor.

I sucked in a breath as his hands found the hem of my shirt and pulled it up and over my head.

He spun me around, my eyes meeting his for a moment, before his gaze dropped to my exposed body. He ran his hands over the curve of my hips. "Fuck, Glory, you're gorgeous."

I didn't see what he did. Not how he saw it, but I was thankful he appreciated me as I was. I reached out and grabbed his belt buckle, undoing it as he pulled his t-shirt over his head.

His abdominals were as defined as ever, and as his pants fell, they revealed a muscled cut v leading to his rock-hard cock. If I'd ever doubted his attraction to me, his stiffness told me otherwise.

Where I was soft, he was hard.

Where my body curved outwards, his dipped in.

We were as opposite in appearance as we were in personality. And yet somehow we *fit*.

I'd always been taller than the average woman, and bigger too, and it was hard to feel feminine because of it. But that wasn't how I felt with Chase. He may have been lean, but he was broad and all-around muscular and strong.

We stepped into the shower together.

The warm water hit my body, soothing my frazzled nerves. Chase's arms were around me again as he rubbed soap all over me. His hand stopped on my right breast, rubbing at my nipple until it pebbled in his palm. He nestled his cock between my ass cheeks as he rinsed the soap off me before his fingers found my clit and massaged it. "I've been listening to you come for months. Imagining that it was me in control of your pleasure. Do you have any idea how that made me feel?"

His fingers dipped down, filling me for the briefest of moments, and I moaned at the penetration. It had been far too long. When he pulled back, I felt emptier than ever. "Frustrated?" I wasn't sure if I was answering his question or telling him how I felt without him inside me.

He put his head next to my ear and, with a gravelly growl, said, "Exactly. But now your body is mine, your pussy is mine, and I'm going to do whatever I want with it." He spun me around, pressing his slick skin against mine. "What do you think about that?"

"I want you to," I said, my voice breathy.

He stroked my cheek, his dark eyes smoldering. "On your knees."

Chapter Fifteen

Chase

I stroked Gloria's cheek, and she opened her mouth. It had been so long since I'd felt any part of her wrapped around my cock, and I was hungry for every part of her. My shaft was rigid with need, with engorged veins popping out, my balls tight and waiting to release into her.

She kissed the tip and smiled up at me, her eyes locked on mine as she sucked it into her mouth. I placed my palm on the shower wall and groaned.

I'd waited so long to be free—to be near her—and despite the events of earlier, I felt like this woman was my home. She took in more of my cock, and I threaded my hand through her damp hair as she bobbed along.

"You look so sexy while wet, baby."

Makeup ran down her face. There was something so raw about the moment. Like it wasn't just the first time we were naked together, but also the first time our hearts had been stripped bare in each other's presence.

With her lips wrapped around it, I watched my cock disappear and reappear from her hot mouth, and flashed back to the first time I'd thought about her while showering in prison. Everything was different now, except for my desire for her.

How was this my reality?

I was a free man and the woman of my dreams was mine.

All fucking mine.

I gripped her hair harder as she sped up.

She took her hand and cupped my balls, giving them a squeeze and, like she'd pressed some button I didn't know I had, I came hard, shooting my load in her mouth. She swallowed it back and smiled up at me before I helped her to her feet.

I brushed the wet hair away from her face, kissing her. "Let's finish up in here, then I'll finish you in the bedroom.

I wrapped Gloria's terry-cloth robe around her and we kissed on our way to the bedroom. I put one knee on the bed and pulled the belt from the loops as I leaned her back onto the mattress.

Her robe fell open. I ran my hand over her breast and down over her hip.

"I can't believe this is my reality. Or that you're mine."

"You better learn to believe it, Chase, because I'm not going anywhere."

"You better believe you're not."

I held the belt from her robe. "Slip off your robe."

She did as she was told, and I grabbed both of her

wrists and lifted them over her head. "Do you remember what I told you about control, Doc?"

"I do. But you don't have to call me that anymore, Chase."

"Oh, but I do."

She smiled as I wrapped the belt around her wrists, tying them to a metal pole on her headboard. "Oh, you do?"

I nodded at her. "It's only right. You got to take advantage of me when my hands were bound. It's my turn to do the same."

"Take advantage?" she laughed. "As if I could ever."

"So you admit I was always in control?"

She pursed her lips. "I see what you did there."

I tickled her midsection, and she flexed, pulling at her bound hands, but they only slid down the pole some. "Chase."

"It's frustrating isn't it, Doc? I wanted to touch you more than anything, but I couldn't. But now—now I can."

I forced her knees apart, and she gasped. I pressed my cock against her pussy, dragging the tip between her slippery folds.

"Did I startle you, Glowbug?"

"No, okay, maybe a little, but I liked it."

There was a knock at Gloria's door. I dropped my voice. "Were you expecting someone?"

"No." Her eyes went wide, and she pulled at the belt.

"Then whoever it is can go away. We've had more than enough intrusions tonight. Now where was I? Oh, right." I pressed the tip of my cock into her. "I was about to fuck you senseless, and there's not a fucking thing you can do about it."

More knocking. Her body went rigid beneath mine.

I grunted. "For fuck's sake, take the damn hint," I said, keeping my voice low.

"Gloria, open up!" A woman's voice called through the door.

Glory exhaled and relaxed back into the bed. "It's my sister, Victoria. We should answer it. She works at the hospital. She may have heard about Lucian or what happened here."

Fuck.

I sat back. "Yeah, you're right. This isn't the best first impression to make." I pointed at her, naked and tied to the bed. "We'll take a raincheck?"

"I liked where this was going."

I smiled down at her, giving her a kiss before freeing her hands, and we dressed. As she walked toward the door, I grabbed her wrist, pulled her back to me and gave her a kiss on the top of the head.

She looked up at me and smiled before pressing a soft kiss on my lips. "Ready?"

"As I'll ever be."

She opened the door and her sister pulled her into an immediate hug. "What took you so long to answer? I hurried over as soon as I heard what happened."

"Breathe Vic, I'm fine."

"A man got shot in your apartment. How are you fine?"

Gloria turned to me. "Because Chase was here."

Victoria's head snapped to look at me and she sucked in a sharp breath. "This is him then?"

Gloria nodded.

"Well, if this is the element you're going to be bringing around here, you better pack your things and get the hell out."

"No, no," Gloria said, "No, you've got it all wrong. Axel came for me, Vic. If Chase hadn't shown up, anything could have happened. The guy in the hospital is Lucian, Chase's friend. He helped me escape and Axel's gun shot him."

"Oh, wow, I—I'm sorry." Victoria said, looking over at me. "I shouldn't have jumped to conclusions."

"It's okay, ma'am. You were just looking out for someone you love. I can understand that."

She smiled at me. "What took you two so long to answer the door, anyhow?"

Gloria burst out laughing and Victoria's face fell when she realized why. She spun in a circle. "I—I should get going. Let you two have your privacy. I have another shift in eight hours and I need to catch some sleep."

"We're going to be heading back to Arizona in the morning. Chase has—" Gloria paused. She was talking about the appointment I had with my parole officer. "He has something urgent he needs to attend to. Do you mind checking in on Lucian for us? They won't tell us much, but I figured you could let us know if he's going to pull through all right."

"Yeah, I can do that. It was nice to meet you, Chase. Thanks for keeping my sister safe."

"No need to thank me." I moved closer to Gloria. "There's nothing I wouldn't do for her."

Victoria smiled. "Then maybe I should welcome you to the family instead?"

Gloria stepped between us. "Okay, you can go now."

I chuckled. "It was nice meeting you too, Victoria."

She slipped out of Gloria's apartment.

"Well, that went better than I expected," Gloria said and turned to me. "It seems I'm not the only Moore that finds you charming."

I cleared my throat. "About that, Glowbug. Something your sister said has got me thinking."

"About what?"

"Why don't we make this official? Make us official, I mean."

"Are you asking me to marry you, Mr. Franklin?"

"I am. Look, I don't have a ring or anything yet, but I'll get it for you, I promise."

"That doesn't matter, Chase. But when you do, and I know you'll make good on your promise, because you always do. I'll cherish it."

Was she saying what I thought she was? "Was that a yes, baby?"

"Are you kidding me? Of course, it was. There's no one else for me other than you. I recognized something special in you from the very first moment we met and you've shown me a love I could have only ever dreamed of."

I wrapped my arms around her and pulled her close. "All my life I was chasing glory. I thought it would come in the form of a medal or a badge of honor. But when all of that slipped through my fingertips, I thought I had nothing else left—until I found you. And if I had it to do over, I'd throw it all away again." I cupped her cheek in my palm. "The moment I laid eyes on you, I knew the hunt was over. Having you. Loving you. Being loved by you. It's more than enough for one man. Because you, Gloria, you're all the glory I'll ever need."

Epilogue

Gloria

Four Years Later

"Come on, Chase, let's go!"

He came around the corner toting our three-year-old daughter, Jasmine, on his hip. She giggled, tugging at his hair.

He wore it longer than he used to. I think the years of being in the military and prison wore on him because right after his release, he let it grow out, leaving the buzz cut behind.

Sometimes I missed the feel of it, but I wasn't complaining. My husband looked even sexier because of the sense of self-pride he wore.

"You need to put her down, my love," I said.

They both turned to me and in unison said, "No." Jasmine had inherited her father's powerful will.

Most of the time, I was thankful that our daughter would grow up as a force to be reckoned with. But I didn't care for it when I was trying to get her to eat something she didn't want to or do anything she might've decided wasn't a part of her own personal agenda. Including letting go of her daddy when it was time to.

"Your Auntie Liberty is going to be here to pick you up soon. You want to see your cousin, Hope, don't you?"

Jasmine's jaw dropped, and she looked at Chase with wide eyes. He laughed. "I told you we had a surprise for you today."

"Put me down, Daddy," she said, and he did before she sauntered over to the entranceway.

He followed her, watching as she put her shoes on the wrong feet, knowing better than to interfere with her concentration.

She pulled them on and stood up, shuffling her feet. "My shoes broke."

He smiled at her and crouched down. "Not broken, Jaz, just misbehaving. Here." He pulled her shoes off and put them on the correct feet.

It warmed my heart watching my huge husband bend his will for our tiny tot. Being a father and protector came more naturally to him than any other role I'd ever seen. When she got hurt, he tended to squeeze between us and tend to the wounds himself.

When we'd found out I was pregnant, we made the move to Weston to be closer to his sister and her family.

Chase had gone to work for Nico. If it wasn't his dream to landscape, he never gave me any sign. Nico and Chase had rekindled the close friendship they had growing up, and the business was booming because of their ongoing hard work.

The doorbell rang, and Chase checked the peephole

before unlocking it. We hadn't seen or heard from Axel in years, yet we stayed vigilant. But with each passing year, it became clearer that it was all behind us.

"Hey, Lib," he said.

"Hey." She turned her attention to Jasmine and held her hand out. "Are you ready for a sleepover?"

Chase lifted the little, pink duffle bag onto his shoulder and hoisted Jasmine up into his free arm.

He carried our child more often than not while he was around, even though she was more than capable of walking by herself.

"Thanks for taking her, Liberty," I said.

She smiled. "Anytime. I hope you two have fun on your getaway."

"Oh, we will," Chase said, waggling his eyebrows before ushering Liberty back through the door following behind with Jasmine.

I'd already packed the car for the drive to Tucson.

We'd be meeting Lucian at the airport for a couple's trip to Hawaii. His girlfriend was flying out of Seattle and meeting us there.

Chase came back into the house, kicked off his boots, and headed straight for me. His powerful arms wrapped around me, his hands sliding down to my behind, squeezing it before he kissed me, and whispered into my ear, "Tell me there's enough time for us to get naked."

"There will be plenty of time for that in Hawaii. But we have to make our flight first."

My insatiable husband groaned as I pried his hands from my backside.

I stepped back. "Come along." I curled my finger, beckoning him to follow me. The familiar heat pooled in his eyes as he raked his teeth over his lower lip.

I led him down the hall. Stopping with my back against

the door. "Okay, let's go," I said, spinning on my heels and darting into the garage.

He reached out to me, but I was too quick and he shook his head. "You'll get as good as you give if you want to tease, you know?"

I looked over my shoulder at him and smiled. "Do you promise?"

<hr>

Chase

"Explain this to me one more time. Why didn't she come?" I asked Lucian. He was wearing a muscle shirt that showed off the scar from that night.

We'd arrived in Hawaii where he was supposed to meet up with the woman he'd been seeing, but she was a no show. When Luc landed and turned on his cell phone, he got the message that she was breaking up with him.

He nodded his head and sighed, "It was a long time coming. But I kind of thought this trip would be our chance to rekindle things. I guess not."

Gloria and I looked at one another. I knew what she was thinking.

There goes our romantic week.

Lucian slapped me on the back. "But don't worry. I'll be out of your hair in no time."

I followed his line of sight. There was a woman across the hotel lobby in tears.

"The crying one?"

He nodded. "You bet. She looks like she could use some cheering up, and I'm a pretty cheerful guy. If all else fails, we can fuck the pain away together."

Glory's mouth fell open, and I knew she had something

to say about that. But when she locked eyes with me, it snapped shut.

"I'll catch you later," Lucian said before wandering off.

Glory shook her head. "That's not healthy."

"He'll be fine," I laughed. "He's survived a lot worse than spending a week cheering up a tearful woman." I knew that he'd do just that. "Besides, do you remember that time your sister interrupted us? We never made up for that. Now's our chance."

Gloria laughed, "Chase, we've made up for that about a thousand times at this point."

I tipped my head. "But have we made up for it *while* in Hawaii?"

"We've never been to Hawaii before."

"Exactly." I stretched my arm around her shoulders and kissed her on the cheek. "Now let's get the hotel room key. I'm sure they have a robe in there somewhere."

Gloria

"You better keep your hands above your head." Chase bound my hands together.

They'd nailed the hotel headboard to the wall, so he wasn't able to tie me to it like he had the night of our reunion.

He stood over me. His huge, hulking presence might have intimidated those who didn't know him like I did or know how squishy he was on the inside for me and our daughter.

"I'm a mother, Chase. I'm on vacation for the first time in years. If you want me to lie here and do nothing, that's a dream come true."

"Good girl. I want you to be as relaxed as you can be for me. Can you tell how much I want you? I've wanted you all fucking day."

He pressed his fingers into me deep, filling me for only a few moments before trailing them up my chest to my throat, over my chin before circling his finger on my lip. "Clean them."

I ran my tongue around his fingers, and between them, before taking them into my mouth, filling it with the tangy taste of myself.

"Do you see how good you taste when you're wet for me, baby? Do you understand why I can't get enough of you, Gloria?"

He kneeled on the bed next to me and gave his cock a few pumps until the tip glistened with pre-cum. He swiped the tip with his thumb and smeared it on my lips. "Lick it off. Only good girls who do what they're told get rewards. Prove to me you're my good girl."

I ran my tongue over my lips while staring into his eyes. This man held all of my heart, and not a day went by that he didn't engulf my body with passion for him.

He ran his hand back down my body, his touch light, causing my back to arch. "Fuck, I've been wanting this all day. Good girls deserve rewards, right?"

I nodded.

"And you're the best fucking girl I know. You always have been. You're dirty for me, but good in every other way. And that's why I can't get enough of you or this pussy."

He ran his fingers between my folds, found my clit, and circled it. I was aching to be filled by him, but I knew by the dance of mischief in his eyes, he was looking to draw this one out.

Maybe I needed to give him some more encouragement. "What's my reward? Are you going to fill me?"

He paused, a smirk grew on his face. "Oh, now you're the one who can't wait? That's interesting, considering you made me wait all fucking day to get you naked. I told you I'd get you back for it. Consider this payback, my love."

I moaned, and he pulled his hand away. "I think you're enjoying that a little too much."

"No, please, don't stop." He moved his body between my legs and grabbed a fistful of my hair. I could feel the outline of his hard cock pressed against me and I lifted my hips to meet him and coax him inside. "No, not yet, baby. You shouldn't have fucking teased me if you're weren't willing to be teased back." He tipped my head back and bit at my neck.

I whimpered at the feel of his teeth and the scratch of his stubble on my sensitive skin. "We were going to be late. I wanted you, Chase. I always want you."

"How much do you fucking want me, Gloria?"

"So much."

"I'm not convinced. Tell me how fucking bad you want my cock."

I wished my hands were free. He wouldn't be able to resist me if my hands were roaming his body. Stroking his shaft until he couldn't help but unload it in me. "I want you to fuck me, Chase. Fuck me now."

He grinned at me, revealing his deep dimple. Using his free hand as a guide, he positioned his cock at my opening and stopped. "Then you're going to take all of me." He released my hair and found my throat, squeezing it as he slammed into me.

I cried out, "Oh, oh yes, keep going." I wrapped my legs around his hips, locking his body between them for leverage to meet his hard and fast pumps with the brace of my hips. I gripped the pillow with my bound hands as he rocked my body with his powerful thrusts.

He reared back, grabbed my legs, and pried them from him. "Don't forget who's in control." He lifted my legs over his shoulders and leaned into me, pinning me against the bed.

I couldn't move. All I could do was lie there and take every inch of his hard cock as he drove it into me.

"Fuck, I love your pussy. Tell me it's mine."

"It's yours. My pussy is yours."

"I'm going to fill you again and by the time this vacation is over, you're going to have another one of my babies inside you. Do you understand me? I'm going to fuck you as often as I want and wherever I want this week."

I panted, my body trembling as it teetered on the brink of climax.

"That's a good girl. Let go. Come on my cock right now."

My body shook as the tension unleashed through my limbs.

He groaned, "That's it now. You're going to take my cum. Every drop of it." He dropped his head and bore his cock as deep into me as he could and when he did, a shock of delicious pain lashed out through me as he battered my cervix before he filled me with his hot seed.

When our combined ecstasy subsided, he untied my hands. "Now get dressed. There's a luau tonight and it starts in twenty minutes."

"Shouldn't we shower first?"

"And wash away my cum? No way." He leaned forward, kissing me. "It'll be our dirty little secret. And your job is to keep that cum inside you tonight. Squeeze your pussy as tight as you can for as long as you can. And if you feel it slip out, you need to tell me. So I can fill you again."

"You weren't kidding about trying to get me pregnant, were you?"

"No, Glory. I'm a man on a mission and failure is not an option."

Thank you for reading, and I hope you enjoyed Chase and Gloria's story.

Are you craving more forbidden age-gap romance reads? Return to Weston for Chase's sister, Liberty's story, Where Liberty Dwells, from the Heart of a Wounded Hero series.

Keep up with me and my couples, updates, future releases, and giveaways, by visiting
https://sendfox.com/literarylovepotions

Or visit **www.literarylovepotions.com/freebies** for bonus content related to this story and more.

Much Love,

Lia

Where Liberty Dwells

HEART OF A WOUNDED HERO

CHAPTER ONE

Liberty

"You're dating *him* again?"

As Nico shook his head, a lock of dark hair fell into his eyes. Though, his expression remained neutral I sensed a storm brewing behind it.

Maybe.

He stuffed his hands in his pockets and looked away as we walked in downtown Tucson, past an inner city park that might have been nice if not for the dried-up fountain, sun-crisped greenery, and worn-out gazebo.

Nico had two ways of being, tough to read and impossible to read.

I bit my lip, not knowing how to respond, or if I was even meant to. Or maybe I was trying to avoid the conversation I dreaded having with him most.

There was a lot to consider, and I knew Nico wouldn't understand, but I wanted to try. "I think Paul has changed.

He hasn't dated since we broke up and he says he misses me and he's sorry."

Nico scoffed. "I don't trust him and neither does Chase. He cheated on you, Libby."

Shame washed over me, but I couldn't keep myself from glancing over at him. He was twenty-nine, young looking and towered over me. It was no wonder he joined the Army and was about to start training for the Ranger's. His body was both lean and strong, built for agility and combat. What *was* a mystery was how he was both pretty and manly looking at the same time. It's alarming how easy on the eyes he was.

Alarming because I'd known *of* Nico my entire life, though from a distance. He'd been my older brother's best friend for decades. I'd not seen much of him until recent years because his father moved them around depending on where he was stationed. But the bond Nico and Chase shared never wavered. They maintained their friendship mostly through online games, and it strengthened even more when Nico moved back to Tucson four years ago. When they tired of working dead-end jobs and enlisted together at twenty-five-years old.

I should have felt out of place as a 20-year-old woman hanging out with her much older brother and his group of Army friends, but I didn't. And out of everyone, Nico and I'd become inseparable, a fact that hadn't escaped Chase, who'd issued us a very stern warning a month prior to *not* get involved. Then again, Chase didn't approve of any guy who wanted to date me.

Still, I didn't let that stop me from hanging out with Nico, and considering we didn't live in the best neighborhood, Chase didn't mind that he escorted me places. But as much as I loved spending time with Nico, I needed to spend *more* time with guys I *could* date. I looked skyward and hoped the clouds looming over us weren't a bad omen brought on by my recent decision to give my ex-boyfriend a second chance.

A crack of thunder roared overhead, followed by an instant rain shower.

Okay, that had to be a bad omen.

Nico grabbed my elbow and pulled me through the nearest park gateway.

"Run," he said, pointing toward the dilapidated gazebo to our right.

We both jogged to evade the fat droplets. I stumbled up the steps, and he reached out for me, pulling me to him. My chest heaved against his, but I was alone in my labored breaths from our dash for shelter. He was far more fit than I was. I looked down at my white cropped t-shirt to see it had turned translucent from the rain, revealing the crimson lace bra I wore beneath. He followed my eye line and sucked in a breath before taking a half-step back.

I laughed and brushed the now wet lock of hair out of his eyes. "One of us should start carrying an umbrella."

He smirked. "As if it'll matter now. I'll be gone soon and you'll be seeing someone."

Frowning, I pulled at my shirt, hoping to hide my bra —it didn't help. "It won't be like that. I know you're my brother's best friend, but you're important to me. I'll always make time for you."

"Yeah, if you say so, Lib." He paused. "I'm sorry. It's not that I don't believe you. It's just that I don't believe it for a fucking second that the prick has changed. I want to see you happy with someone. But my gut is telling me it won't be with him. Besides, when Chase finds out, he's going to rough him up. You know that. He still hasn't forgiven him, and never will." He huffed. "Neither will I."

So far, our conversation was going about as well as I suspected it would.

I sat down cross-legged on the wooden slatted floor of the gazebo. He pulled off his leather jacket and sat down next to me, hanging it over my shoulders as we looked out toward the fountain in the middle of the clearing. I traced the surrounding path with my eyes before leaning my head on his arm.

He had to be wrong.

Paul wouldn't dare put me through that all over again, would he? But what if he did?

I was already nervous about Nico's upcoming training and deployment. He'd become my rock in a very short amount of time. He was different from the other guys in the group. There was a seriousness about him that made him stand out. If I ever needed anyone to talk to about anything, he was my go to. Could I really face another failed relationship attempt without him? If it didn't work out with Paul it would be Nico that I would want to console me. It was his guidance I would want above anyone else's. His shoulder I'd want to lean my head on when uncertainty weighed heavily on my mind. It made my skin prickle to think it, but I had to let go of that feeling. It wasn't fair to either of us.

Yes, dating Paul might turn out to be a bad idea. But unlike Nico, I wasn't a six-foot stoic god of a man that could have had any woman *if* he wanted her. I was just a five-foot-five girl with a cute face (so I'd been told), and more curves than most guys seemed to know what to do with. Or maybe I was kidding myself and they were more curves than most guys wanted.

Either way.

I needed love, and sure Paul wasn't perfect, but it was better than the alternative of sitting around and waiting for some Prince Charming to come whisk me off my feet. No, waiting wasn't an option. I wanted to date. To fall in love and experience the entire whirlwind of emotions that came along with it. Even if getting back together with Paul was foolish, I needed to take the chance rather than live life wondering what *may* have been.

Nico turned his head, kissing the top of mine. A rare gesture from him. The last time it happened was when my mother passed the year before and both he and Chase came home for a couple of weeks of rest and relaxation. Losing Mom was tough. I think that's why Chase took me under his wing like he did. He just wanted to make sure that without her around, I'd be okay. And I was, thanks to Chase and, later, Nico.

The head kiss confused me, though, because I didn't need comforting, or I shouldn't have. I was starting a new relationship. It should have been an exciting time. So why did I feel like the dark clouds weren't only looming in the sky that night, but between Nico and I? Was he—no, he couldn't be—why did it feel like he was kissing me goodbye?

A lump formed in my throat as I looked up at him. He dropped his eyes, looking back at me. His lip twitched into the faintest smile, revealing an almost never seen but highly sought after dimple. He only had the one, but then again he only ever half-smiled, at most, so maybe there was another one hidden behind that stubble that I'd never seen. There was something so bittersweet about the moment that my chest ached in abstract longing.

He sighed. "I want you to know I'll always be around…"

"Why do I sense there's a 'but' coming?"

He groaned and dropped his arm from my shoulders.

"Because you know me. Even better than I know myself sometimes."

I shook my head. "You don't have to do this, you know."

"Neither do you. But you're doing it. And I won't watch. No, I *can't* watch. If you're going to go back to Paul, you'll be facing it alone. I can't watch the woman I—" He paused. "—my best friend's little sister self-destruct."

"Don't. Just don't. Why are you doing this? I'll be okay. I'm older now. Stronger. Wiser. I can handle myself. Just, please, don't pull away from me."

"Do you want to know why?"

"I do." My phone buzzed, and I reached into my purse, pulling it out. The caller id flashed Paul's name. I set it on my thigh, still ringing. I'd call him back in a minute.

Nico grabbed my chin, tipped my head up to him, and placed a firm kiss on my lips.

What the…

My chest thudded with panic, stealing my breath away. I looked down at the still buzzing phone with Paul's name taunting me on it. Guilt washed over me.

Nico hopped up. "That's why."

"Nico, I—"

He cut me off and pointed at the phone. "And you may as well take that. Because we both know that's what you want to do."

My jaw went slack. I didn't know what I wanted to do. On the one hand, I'd waited a couple of years for Paul to say the things he'd told me earlier that day. It felt like vindication. But I'd never imagined Nico and I would become as close as we had. Or that he would feel any kind of way about me, let alone want to kiss me.

The phone kept buzzing. I looked down at it and back up at Nico. Speechless. Why did he wait until now to do this? Did he want me, or was he just trying to keep me from seeing Paul again?

He ripped the phone from my lap with a growl and pressed answer. "For fuck's sake, man, we'll be there in a few," he said and hung up the phone before tossing it into my lap. I'd never heard him bark out at anyone like that before. He crossed his arms over his chest, biceps popping out. "Well?"

"Well, what? What do you expect me to say now?"

"Anything. Something. Tell me to fuck off or that you never want to see me again. Tell me you can't date him now. Or, shit, tell me you feel the same way. Fucking anything, Lib! Anything to put me out of my misery."

"What misery? This is the first I'm learning of this. You never seem miserable around me." The rain started easing up, fewer and fewer droplets disturbing the surface of the small puddle that had developed in a dip in the pavement just outside the gazebo.

"That's because I'm around *you*. Why not choose me? Tell me why?"

"I don't know. I didn't think this was on the table for us. What about Paul? Or Chase? He'll lose his mind if he hears about this. Have you thought about that?"

He nodded. "That's a lot of excuses you have at the ready. You're right then. It isn't on the table for us. Forget I did that." He reached out his hand to me. "Come on, let's get out of here before the rain starts up again. I'll walk you, but I'm skipping the party. I've embarrassed myself enough for one night." He pulled me to my feet.

"You haven't. Please come."

"Can't."

"Why not?"

"Because Paul's going to be there and if I see him lay one fucking hand on you, or even smile in your general direction, I'll knock his teeth out. Is that something you want?"

"Well, no, but…"

"Then you go alone. Do what you've gotta do."

I wanted to just throw caution to the wind. To tell Nico that I thought we had a chance. That Chase *might* accept us. But I didn't believe it. He was bad enough about me dating guys my age. There was no telling how he'd react if I dated his best friend who was pushing thirty.

Even knowing all of that, a part of me wanted to stay right there and sort it out with Nico. Maybe we could work it out? But Paul was waiting for me. We were already forty-five minutes late. It all felt so overwhelming. And even if by some miracle I could choose Nico, I at least needed to go end it with Paul. If that was even what I wanted to do. Nico and I both needed a bit of time to reflect before taking things any further. At least, I knew I did. "Okay, let's go, then." We stepped out of the gazebo, walking through the park, before starting back down the road. The rain reduced to a drizzle.

I glanced over at him and he returned my gaze through thick dark lashes and for the first time, my heart swelled in a new way for him. A way that I couldn't accept without consequence.

Had I known he'd stop taking my calls and move away, I would have skipped the party, and that's what I should have done.

But I *didn't*.

And that was the last time I thought I'd ever see Nico Andino.

CHAPTER TWO

Nico

FIVE YEARS LATER

I parked my truck out front of the white a-frame in the historic district. The neighborhood was the last piece of Weston's suburbs left untouched by developers and their oversized modern homes. The area would have been a developer's dream if not for soft ground that ran the length of the backyards, rendering half of each property unstable. I'd had more than a couple of build permits declined in the neighborhood.

My assistant, Cody, hopped out of the truck ahead of me. He was always eager to impress and way more of a morning person than I was. I took a few more sips of coffee before meeting him at the tailgate. "You grab the gear. I'll go have a chat with the homeowner."

Abby, my office manager, said the job order was for an addition on the house. A sunroom, to be exact. But there was a problem. I was looking right at one. She must have got her wires crossed. Maybe we were removing it?

Fuck, I hoped not.

It would have been a shame to do anything to the house that ruined its original character.

I walked up the path toward the well-maintained home. The glass was new and the structure sound. It was looking like they might be another pain-in-the-ass homeowner with ridiculous expectations. But, it was nothing new. It was the life I'd built for myself after my injury forced me out of the military. And, I was damn proud of what I'd built. Still, the house was just about as nice as it could be for its age. Any changes would've messed with perfection at that point.

I knocked before noticing the doorbell and pressed it for good measure.

A muffled woman's voice called out from inside. "Coming."

I turned, looking past the manicured lawn and down the street at the row of old houses. The sun was high in the Arizona sky. It was another blistering hot one.

Then again, when wasn't it?

The door creaked open behind me. "Hi, sorry to keep you waiting."

I turned to face her and took one step forward before stopping. Wide, blue eyes and a cascade of brown hair framed her heart-shaped face, a smear of clear gloss topped her full, kissable lips. Lips that adorned a face too familiar to forget. "Liberty?"

What was she doing here? When had she moved to Weston from Tucson? I leaned back and checked the house number. 765. I had the correct address. There was no doubting that.

"Nico!" She stepped forward out of her house wearing a white terry cloth robe tied tight around her waist, accentuating her generous hourglass shape, and gave me a tight hug.

I stood still.

As still as a stone statue.

Unable to return the gesture out of sheer shell-shock. "It must be my lucky day. Yours was the first construction company I called. And I didn't even know it. Small world, isn't it?" She rattled on, weaving a strand of chestnut hair through her fingertips.

"It sure is. When did you move here?" Something about the situation made me think it was anything but a coincidence, but I played along.

She stepped back into the house and motioned for me to come in. "Three weeks ago. I'm still getting settled, so don't mind the mess." I crossed the threshold into her living area. What mess? There were only a few boxes stacked along one wall.

I ran my hand through my hair. "Abby said you needed a sunroom? But—" I pointed over my shoulder.

She chewed at her bottom lip. "It's small."

"It fits the house."

"True, but I pictured more space for greenery."

I laughed. This was coming from the woman that couldn't keep a silk plant alive back in the day.

A wide smile broke out on her face. "I know what you must be thinking."

"So you've learned how to keep plants alive, have you?"

"Yes and no. I've just found the right plants for me. Succulents. Low maintenance, but I need the sun to do the heavy lifting."

I furrowed my brow. "How many succulents does one woman need?"

"Enough for my fairy gardens?"

Well, now I'd heard it all. "What in the world is that?"

"My business. Come, let me show you." She led me through the house and out the sliding glass door that led into the backyard. There was a table with several ceramic planters filled with scenes. Houses made of logs, tiny glass toadstools, little wooden swing sets and blue stone ponds. All miniatures with clusters of succulents arranged among them.

"Wow," I said. Although, it didn't surprise me one bit that she'd chosen to do something like that. Minus the plants, that is. "Geez, when I left, you were studying to be an accountant."

She scrunched up her nose. And she might as well have just hurled a dagger at my heart because I'd let myself forget how freaking cute she looked when she did that.

"It wasn't for me."

"I could have told you that." And, I had. But the thing about Liberty was that she loved exploration. It was just hard to tell her that maybe every fleeting interest didn't *need* to become a career. Or that she could take an interest in something without having to throw herself headlong into it.

She blinked. "So yeah, I need some more plant space. It's cheaper to grow my own than it is to buy everything from a nursery. Can you help me?"

I looked out at the spacious backyard. "How about this? We leave the house as is because you'll be kicking yourself if I put some big eyesore of a sunroom on it. And instead we build you a greenhouse? It'll be cheaper too. Not as many materials needed and if we keep it modest, there's no need for a permit."

She threw her hands up. "Now why hadn't I thought about that?"

Because she rarely thought things through? Or at least that used to be true. But I'd loved that about her. How unpredictable she could be.

Until it hadn't worked in my favor.

I shrugged. "I'll get my assistant in here. We'll take some measurements and I'll draw up some schematics tonight for your approval in the morning."

"Sounds perfect. Coffee tomorrow then?"

I paused. Caught up in the subtle pout of her lips as she waited for my reply. I swallowed hard.

Her eyes went wide. "To go over the schematics, of course."

"Uh yeah, sure, coffee'd be great." My eyes dropped to her hands. No wedding ring. I heard that she'd married that idiot Paul and divorced him a few years later. A five-year-old anger simmered in me like a pot coming to a boil. He'd fucked up again, hadn't he?

"Nico? Are you okay?"

She knew as well as I did that I wasn't.

At least, not *yet*.

None of this was okay. Her moving to my town. Me showing up on her doorstep. It was the furthest thing from 'okay'. I'd thought about how it would feel to see her, but not knowing her intentions made things harder. All it did was make me register my loss all over again, and wish that things could have been different and that we could get back the years we'd wasted.

Or, better yet, that I'd gone to that party with her and knocked his teeth out like I said I would. Because then maybe it would have prevented whatever heartbreak brought her here…

To me.

That was the bottom line, wasn't it? She could try to pass this off as a coincidence as much as she liked, but she was in Weston because it was over with him and it wasn't with *me* yet. The question was, for what purpose? I'd told her, that last night, that I'd always be there for her. That I was only out of her life as long as she was with him. And even then I hadn't planned on keeping my word because I hadn't planned on staying away from her period. But when I'd gone to Chase and told him what had happened and how I felt about Liberty, all I got was a black eye and told to 'stay the fuck away from my little sister'. I could have fought back, and won, had I not respected the guy so much. That my love for her pushed me to cross the line at all with him spoke volumes. There was no way I'd be okay with standing on the sidelines again as I watched her carry on with the next idiot.

The only thing that was for sure was that I'd have a few days of construction time to figure it out.

"Seriously, Nico, are you okay?"

"I'm better than I've been in years, Lib." And standing across from her it was true. As much confusion as I might have felt, I couldn't ignore the fact that it was my chance. My chance to get what I'd always wanted. To prove to Liberty just how well I could love her. Whether Chase approved was irrelevant to me. We hadn't talked since I made it into the Rangers and he didn't and blew up at me.

Cody came around the side of the house. "There you are."

I introduced them before informing him of the change of plans. "Get your measuring tape out."

Liberty smiled. "I'll go get you two something cold to drink. It's too warm out."

I put up my hand, stopping her. "Save it for tomorrow. We won't be long today."

Her smile faltered. "Oh, that's right."

"But we'll be back tomorrow." Or at least I would. I wasn't about to pass up the opportunity to get one-on-one time with her. Besides, I only needed Cody around once the construction began. My back couldn't handle all the crouching or kneeling anymore.

She tried to contain her smile and gave me a nod. I didn't know what tomorrow would bring, but I felt I wasn't alone in hoping it would be something good.

I hope you enjoyed this sample. You can find the rest of Nico & Liberty's story, Where Liberty Dwells on Amazon or visit:
books2read.com/wherelibertydwells

Also by Lia Preston

RELATED BOOKS

WHERE LIBERTY DWELLS

JOIN CHASE'S SISTER, LIBERTY, ON HER STEAMY SECOND-CHANCE ROMANCE JOURNEY WITH HER BROTHER'S BEST FRIEND, NICO.

HERE GHOST NOTHING

RETURN TO WESTON FOR ANOTHER WOUNDED HERO TALE AND MEET EX-FIREFIGHTER, ZANE, FOR HIS SECOND-CHANCE WITH PIPER.

MAN ON A *MISSION* SERIES

MISS CONDUCT

JOIN PAIGE AND HER SILVER FOX BOSS, RHYS, ON THEIR SPICY FORBIDDEN ROMANTIC JOURNEY.

MISS EDUCATION

JOIN ELLE AND HER SEXY IRISH PROFESSOR, FINN, ON THEIR KINKY FORBIDDEN ROMANTIC JOURNEY.

MISS FORTUNE

JOIN BRIDGET AND HER BEST FRIEND'S BROTHER, HUNTER, ON THEIR SPICY SECOND-CHANCE FORBIDDEN ROMANCE JOURNEY.

About the Author

Lia Preston is an author of short contemporary romances. She loves writing body-positive stories about curvy heroines in forbidden romance scenarios with their sizzling hot alpha heroes.

She was diagnosed with ADHD as an adult and aims to provide readers with quality romance stories that cater to shorter attention spans, busier lifestyles, or those who need a palate cleanser between longer reads.

She has much more in store for her readers and can't wait to share it all over the coming years. If you're a fan of paranormal or sci-fi romance, Lia has a fantasy fanatic alter ego, Luna Preston, and will be releasing her debut in early 2023.

Visit **www.literarylovepotions.com** for more information.

amazon.com/author/liapreston

facebook.com/literarylovepotions

instagram.com/literary_love_potions

bookbub.com/authors/lia-preston

tiktok.com/@literary_love_potions